# THE
# DEVIL'S
# RANGE

Center Point
Large Print

Also by Lee E. Wells and available from Center Point Large Print:

*The Naked Land*
*Tarnished Star*
*Treachery Pass*
*Vulture's Gold*

**This Large Print Book carries the Seal of Approval of N.A.V.H.**

# THE DEVIL'S RANGE

## LEE E. WELLS

CENTER POINT LARGE PRINT
THORNDIKE, MAINE

This Center Point Large Print edition
is published in the year 2017 by arrangement with
Golden West Literary Agency.

First US edition: Berkley

The text of this Large Print edition is unabridged.
In other aspects, this book may vary
from the original edition.
Printed in the United States of America
on permanent paper.
Set in 16-point Times New Roman type.

ISBN: 978-1-68324-590-2 (hardcover)
ISBN: 978-1-68324-594-0 (paperback)

Library of Congress Cataloging-in-Publication Data

Names: Wells, Lee E., 1907-1982, author.
Title: The devil's range / Lee E. Wells.
Description: Center Point large print edition. | Thorndike, Maine :
    Center Point Large Print, 2017.
Identifiers: LCCN 2017036752| ISBN 9781683245902
    (hardcover : alk. paper) | ISBN 9781683245940 (pbk. : alk. paper)
Subjects: LCSH: Large type books. | GSAFD: Western stories.
Classification: LCC PS3545.E5425 D48 2017 | DDC 813/.54—dc23
LC record available at https://lccn.loc.gov/2017036752

# I

In the six months he had been in Olanthe, Larry Crane had come to accept the daily ceremony of meeting the train, but today it had particular meaning for him. The town was so small that all its citizens could head for the railroad station when the first smudge appeared on the horizon, and be there by the time the locomotive, with its high, triangular funnel belching smoke and sparks like a demon, rolled over the switch at the end of town, and came roaring toward the platform.

More often than not, it roared on, east or west, depending on the day, with a blasting salute of the whistle that smacked off the high false fronts of the line of saloons, gambling halls, and buildings that faced the tracks on the north side. Then the crowd would slowly disperse, the rattling-bang of ornate passenger car, ugly freights, and final caboose in its ears.

There was a schedule posted in the waiting room, but it was more hope than fact. A flood could wash out a trestle in Colorado, or buffalo could stampede across the tracks in Kansas, or Apaches could be loose in New Mexico, or, at any spot, outlaws could pile rocks and logs on the rails. So the little black finger of smoke marked the actual arrival, particularly of trains from the west.

The train from the east was more regular. It had but a hundred chancey miles before it arrived at Olanthe. A man could depend upon it, as Larry Crane did by glancing at the clock on the wall in his office shack, and then at the calendar just below it. Briggs and Whelan should arrive today.

Larry pulled himself from the chair before his roll-top desk, picked his long-skirted, black coat from a peg, and shoved his arms into it, snugging it down over wide, muscular shoulders. He checked his appearance before a heavily-framed mirror above a table by the far wall. He adjusted his string tie, and smoothed the front of his white shirt. He touched a comb to the black hair that waved back from his high forehead. He moved a finger over his long upper lip to make certain his razor had missed nothing that morning. Satisfied, he turned away with a smooth, flowing movement and picked up a black, flat-crowned hat, placed it on his head, and shaped the wide brim at an angle.

He left the office shack, closing but not locking the door behind him. He had not been able to break himself of the habit of a pleased, hopeful look at the goldleaf lettering on the shack's wide single window, which read: LAWRENCE E. CRANE—LAND AGENT—CHICAGO & FAR WESTERN RR.

But today, his gray eyes merely swept over it,

and he turned sharply and started down the short dirt street to the station. He hesitated before Overman's General Store, just across the street, then thought, "I can take care of that later," and moved on.

At the corner, to his left, stood the row of saloons and the town's second hotel-of-sorts, all silent, ugly, and apparently uninhabited. Larry crossed toward the orange-and-black building on the railroad station's platform.

Beyond the station, rails gleamed in the bright afternoon sunlight—the main line and the spur track that served the long row of empty, gaunt stock pens which broke the line of the horizon, its flatness accented by a few scattered cottonwoods. That empty country annoyed Larry. He wanted to fill it, he wanted to make Olanthe into a real town, maybe a county seat.

But thinking of Briggs and Whelan helped his annoyance to pass. His lips formed a low but cheerful whistle as he stepped up on the platform and strode along to the open doorway of the waiting room.

His steps sounded overloud in the empty room; with its unoccupied benches along three walls. An inner door opened, and Ross Gentry peered out. Ross was muscular enough, but he had round shoulders and the long face of a hound, with big, sad eyes. His pepper-and-salt mustache compensated for his baldness.

"Oh, you!" Ross sounded disappointed. "What brings you?"

Larry laughed. "You don't expect *me* to buy a ticket, do you, Ross? I'm meeting the Westbound. It's on time?"

"Maybe for once." Ross came out into the room, closing the door behind him. "Dispatcher at Grayling telegraphed it went through there on the minute."

Larry went outside, and Ross followed him. They looked eastward down the narrowing tracks to the horizon. "Big day for us and the railroad, Ross."

Ross's sad eyes lighted with a flash of memory. "Those two and their families are due in—that's right, ain't it?"

Larry nodded and looked over at the stock pens. Ross said, "They'll be full, soon. I reckon some trail boss will be riding in ahead any day to make sure of pens. Toward the middle of the drive, all that country out there will be full of cattle, waiting for pens and loading."

Ross made a sweeping gesture southward, beyond the pens. "One time of year, I'm busy as a dozen men. Rest of the time, I ain't worth my salary."

"You will be, all the time, when I get through."

Ross gave Larry a covert look. Larry stood at the far corner of the station, hands behind his back, tall and slender, his head lifted, his long face aglow with self-confidence.

Ross shrugged. "Sure. I hope so. Right now, I ain't making any plans more'n expect the beef buyers in from Chicago and Kansas City."

Larry swung his head about sharply. "You know what the railroad plans—all through this country."

"Glad it's your job, not mine. Me, I'll just sell tickets and cattle cars."

Larry started to protest, but both men heard the sound of boots on the platform, and turned around. A man, with a bright nickel badge on his black vest, said "Howdee. It's coming."

He pointed eastward, and they saw a touch of black against pure blue sky. Ross said, "Be damned! It's on time."

In a minute, another man, still wearing his bartender's apron, appeared around the corner of the station. Then a third appeared, and within the next five minutes, a dozen or more. Now, all of them could distinguish a black dot growing under the thickening rise of smoke to the east. More people appeared. Bored women brazenly ogled Larry, who paid no attention. A cadaverous man, with greedy eyes, moved through the small crowd. He ran one of the gambling halls.

Now, the locomotive was growing fast. Portly Harry Overman joined the group, and Larry nodded to him with a smile, but Overman's eyes showed disappointment. The train loomed, and its whistle shattered the dome of the prairie sky.

Gasps of surprise around him brought his attention sharply to the train. It was slowing down, still some distance off. White steam hissed from the sides of the locomotive, like the angry exhalation of a dragon. Marshal Ace Clemson exclaimed, "It's stopping!"

"Beef buyers?" the gambler asked hopefully.

"It'd come into the station," someone objected.

The train stopped just beyond the beginning of the spur line. A man moved up the line of cars. The crowd watched him wrestle the switch around and give a signal. The train crawled forward onto the secondary track fronting the pens. It stopped, and the brakeman cut loose the caboose, grabbed the handrail of the last car, and the train rolled on.

It stopped again, and the last car was uncoupled. The brakeman hurried to the locomotive, stepped up onto the long, pointed cowcatcher, and the train moved the full length of the switch track onto the main line, and backed toward the station.

All heads on the platform had moved with the train, eyes wide open and mouths agape—except for Larry and Ross. Now, the train backed by them without stopping, picked up the caboose, and rolled forward to make its proper stop.

Larry and Ross stepped forward as the conductor swung down off the coach step. Ross accepted a flimsy from the conductor as Larry moved on to greet a man stepping down onto the platform. "Mr. Briggs, welcome to your new home!"

Briggs, a man with a squat, powerful body and round, fleshy face to match, smiled faintly, and accepted Larry's hand with an air of suspicion. Above him on the step, another man appeared, and Larry said, "And you, too, Mr. Whelan."

Whelan was tall, gaunt, all knobs and knees, long of face and with cheeks scored by hard work. But his deep-set eyes glowed appreciation. "Glad to have the trip over, Mr. Crane. Though there's a mighty lot of work still to be done."

Larry became aware of the curious crowd behind him as more people poured out of the single coach. Two women, of a size, and with the prim look of disapproval that covers uncertainty, bobbed bonneted heads to Larry, and were identified as Mrs. Briggs and Mrs. Whelan. Then came two smooth young faces, whose eyes were wide with a mixture of excitement and fright that they manfully tried to conceal. The shorter of the two youths proved to be Luke Briggs, the other Jory Whelan. They were followed by two girls of nine and ten, Briggs' daughters.

Wives, sons, and daughters carried bundles, carpetbags, big, wicker lunch hampers. Briggs and Whelan stood empty-handed, their black suits wrinkled and dust-powdered, their hands in their pockets, staring at the crowd that stared back. The conductor called " 'Board!", a bell

11

clanged, and steam hissed. The train, with a jerk and a clash of couplings, pulled away and rolled westward, almost unnoticed.

Larry said to Briggs, "I've arranged for a place for you to stay."

Blue eyes, above rounded cheeks, glanced to Larry. "All of us? We ain't got much money left, what with all the train tickets, and moving, and such."

"We'll take care of that later," Larry answered, a touch sharply.

He took bundles from the two women, and started along the platform. A scraggly parade formed after him. As Larry passed the marshal, Clemson's heavy-featured face revealed something close to dislike. But nothing was said, and Larry led the way across the barren expanse to the single street, and up it to the Olanthe Hotel.

As he started up the steps to the porch, Kathy Blaine appeared in the doorway. She was a tall, shapely woman with golden hair and blue eyes which were wide at sight of the procession advancing across the porch. Larry drank in the sight of her, lovely framed in the dark doorway, and felt that jump in his heartbeat she had always caused. Kathy recovered, flashed a warm smile of white, even teeth, and made them welcome.

It took some time to get the Briggses and the Whelans registered, sorted, and put in the right rooms. Larry went out on the porch, and dropped into a comfortable rocker. He lazily watched the empty street, and listened to the voices from the lobby. Those voices, those people pleased him, for they were the first concrete step in the long-range job which had been entrusted to him.

His mind moved on into the future, and his eyes narrowed thoughtfully. He did not realize the noise within had faded and then stopped altogether, until Kathy suddenly appeared beside him.

He jumped up. "They're all tagged and tucked away?"

"Yes. We've never had eight guests all at one time before, except during cattle season."

He chuckled. "A foretaste of what will happen. There'll be more, a lot more. Then the drummers will come, and more stores, more business. Great things are about to happen in Olanthe."

She smiled uncertainly, brushing a golden lock from her forehead. "Mother and I are grateful for these, what with the hotel practically empty." A frown shadowed her forehead. "They're the farmers you talked about?"

"The very ones! First of many!"

She looked away, along the street, pursing her red lips. Then she looked back at him. "This is a cattle town—a trail-herd town."

"It is—now. It won't be long," he said shortly.

"I know. You see it that way. But the others?"

"They're blind. They don't see change. They

haven't the br—" He caught himself, amended, "They haven't the imagination to know that change is coming."

Her eyes held his a moment, challenging and yet sadly understanding. "Then give them time, and don't force farmers on them. You're impatient, I think."

"I have to be."

"Why? Or, at least, why show it? It's like telling somebody he's stupid."

His jaw dropped, anger flashed in his gray eyes and then vanished into a chuckle. "Well! You say it right out!"

"Just a warning. I'd hate to see any real nice person get in trouble he could avoid." Her tone changed, and she turned to the door. "With all those extra mouths you brought, Mr. Crane, Mother and I had best get to the kitchen."

She was gone before he could stop her. For a moment, he stood looking at the empty doorway, half amused, half angry. He turned, and looked out on the street. The shadows lengthened, as the sun dipped west. More than an hour until supper. Though Briggs and Whelan might be down any moment, Larry didn't want to discuss their problems right now. He left the porch, and strolled down the street toward the tracks.

The lamps of the big, barn-like Texas Saloon were not yet lit when Larry pushed through the batwings. The huge room echoed his steps,

14

despite a scattering of sawdust. Larry had never seen more than half a dozen townsmen in the place, though he had heard it was jam-packed during the season of the trail crews.

Ace Clemson stood at the long bar, the cadaverous gambler beside him. Bat Owens acted as his own bartender. He was a beefy man, with a round face and thinning, slicked-down hair. He looked up as Larry entered, and the other men watched Larry approach in the back-bar mirror. They didn't turn to greet him, though they did say hello as he came up. Larry had become used to their attitude.

Bat asked, "What'll it be?"

"The usual, and for the gentlemen, too."

Ace half-turned to protest, and then leaned back on his elbow as Bat deftly filled his glass. Dick Poole, the gambler, gave a curt nod of acceptance. The men lifted glasses in silent salute, and downed their drinks.

"A second, gentlemen," Larry suggested, and Bat quickly filled the glasses.

The four men fingered their glasses, taking their time. Ace asked, "Celebrating?"

"In a way. Say, I feel good."

"Them folks," Ace nodded. "Farmers. New breed to these parts."

"You'll get used to them."

Poole tapped his glass with his tapered fingers. "Not so sure. Never heard that farmers play cards, or drink much. What good'll they do us?"

"Not much, from where I stand," Bat rumbled, behind the bar.

"Well, don't worry about it," Ace said easily. "This ain't farming country. Give 'em six months, a year, and they'll go back east—broke."

Larry laughed harshly. "Want to bet?"

"I would," Poole answered as harshly.

"So would I," Ace cut in. "If bad farm land don't break 'em, the Texas punchers will. Something Texas punchers don't like is a damn sodbuster."

"They'll have to like these," Larry shot back. "And a lot more like 'em. The railroad is going to bring 'em in."

"Or you?" Bat asked.

Ace held up a placating hand. "Now let's not argue. Crane does what he sees best, like any of us. It won't work, as he'll find out, but let him learn it."

"What I don't understand is why," Poole complained.

Larry considered them—the marshal, the gambler, and the saloonkeeper. He recalled Marlowe telling him, just before he left Chicago to set up things in this excrescence of a town: "They'll think there's no other way to live than they've lived in the past, Larry. You have to let them know they're wrong. You'll have to explain that the C&FW means more money than they've seen before—and all the year round. They

16

won't believe you—so explain, and explain, and explain. We want no trouble, but we also know what the railroad has to build up, if it's going to live. Might be that the townsmen will get in the way. If they do, too bad—but get 'em on our side, if you can."

Marlowe's memory-voice ceased, and Larry heard Poole's "Why?" again.

Bat, heavy elbows on the bar, nodded approval to Poole, then turned to Larry. "Why you got to bring farmers in?"

Larry clunked his empty glass on the bar. "I've been telling the whole town, for six months. The day of the trail-herds is about over, and—"

"They'll be coming this year, as usual," Poole cut in.

"But maybe not next year—surely not the year after."

Poole frowned darkly. "Because you're going to try to drive 'em away. Well, none of us in Olanthe are going to see our living money driven off by you, the railroad, or anyone else."

Larry asked, "How can you stop what's bound to happen?"

"Because you'll make it happen?" Bat demanded, his beefy fist thudding on the bar.

"Not him," Poole sneered. He pushed from the bar and stood dark, lean, and menacing. "Might as well say right now, Mr. Crane, don't bring in any more of them plowmen."

"Why not?"

Poole's arm made a peculiar jerk, and Larry looked into the muzzle of a derringer. Poole twisted his thin lips into a smile. "Answer enough?"

Ace Clemson dropped his hand on Poole's wrist, knocking the weapon aside and down. He held Poole's wrist, and met Poole's angry eyes calmly.

"Put it up, Dick. None of that, around here. I'll jail you as quick as any drunken cowboy."

Their eyes locked a second, and then Poole shrugged. Cautiously, Ace released Poole's hand, and the derringer dropped into the gambler's wide coat pocket.

Ace turned to Larry. "But I reckon you've had your answer."

# II

Larry was early as usual in getting down to the hotel dining room, next morning. Even so, all the Briggses and Whelans were up before him. They congregated on the sunny porch, the girls making a racket with their playing and squealing.

Larry crossed the lobby into the dining room without their seeing him, and sat down at a table. A moment later, Kathy looked in from the kitchen door. "Good morning. The usual?"

He nodded, smiling, and she disappeared, then returned with a steaming cup of coffee. As she placed it before him, he indicated the group out on the porch. "They came down at least an hour ago," Kathy explained. "How long will they be staying?"

"Another night, at least. I'm taking the men out to their farms, after we've seen Overman."

"Farms—strange word around here."

"It won't be."

She turned and walked away. Frowning, Larry sipped his coffee. Then he shrugged, and his face cleared. Kathy Blaine, he was certain, did not have a knot of wood for a head: she would come around and understand. Feeling better, he tackled the platter of eggs and bacon she served him a few moments later. But she disappeared into the kitchen before he could talk to her.

He was almost finished when Briggs pushed his round head into the lobby doorway. When he saw Larry, he spoke over his shoulder, and came in, Whelan following. They dropped into chairs at the table, without apology.

"Good morning," Larry said.

"Lazy morning, I'd say. Been up and down the street, and they ain't nothing open, or no one moving. Day's 'most half-gone."

"No need to get up before dawn. Not this time of year."

"Get no work done that way."

Larry finished the last of his bacon, and contentedly drank his coffee. Briggs watched. His blue eyes were like clear marbles and, Larry thought, just as revealing. The round, tanned face, though pleasantly open, at first glance, could be secretive, at a second, and Larry realized he had not seen a real smile on Briggs' thick, pursy lips.

"When we going to get things moving?" Briggs demanded. "Day's wasting."

Larry remained unruffled, and sipped his coffee as Briggs watched, disapproving. Briggs cleared his throat to speak again, but Larry saw Kathy and signaled her over with the big, granite pot. She refilled his cup, and Larry asked, "Gentlemen?"

Whelan slanted an apologetic look at Briggs as he said, "If the lady has more. Couldn't sleep a wink last night, what with a strange town and a whole bunch of things on my mind."

Kathy brought him a mug, filled it, and departed. Briggs leaned back in his chair and folded his stubby arms. His face was set. "Always heard time was money."

"I believe it," Larry agreed. "Since no store's open yet, I'm spending a few pennies of it." He turned to Whelan. "What bothered you so you couldn't sleep?"

"Mainly everything that's to be done—and how much it'll cost."

Larry leaned forward, suddenly all business. "I've told you the deal, Mr. Whelan. You—and Mr. Briggs—will get every support the railroad can give you. Your land purchase is on a long-term mortgage, at low interest. Your hotel bill here will be paid by us until such time as you can move out to your farms. You've brought your farming equipment out, at railroad expense. It's sitting in that boxcar alongside the cattle pens right now."

"But there's a lot more to be bought—tools, horses, food —things like that."

"The railroad is aware of that. You'll get 'em."

"But they cost!"

"That's right. The railroad—I told you this, weeks ago, when you came out and bought the land, remember?—will advance the money. In fact, lumber for your houses and barns is out

21

at the siding right now, in that car with your equipment. You pay us back, starting a year from now, and extending over two more years."

He eased back with a smile. "Now what's there to worry about?"

"We know all about the deal, Mr. Crane. You going to do that for everyone that comes to farm out here?"

"No—maybe two or three more families, that's all. If we can help five farms get established in Olanthe, those five will bring in five more—and the ten, ten more, we hope. That's more land sold, and that's all we want."

Briggs gave a pinched, triumphant smile. "Not quite all, Mr. Crane. In the contract, it says anything we ship out goes by C&FW Railroad, and no other way."

"What other way is there?"

"Team and wagon, for one."

"You'd be a fool. It'd cost more than our shipping charges. No, Mr. Briggs, we feel that if we help you, as we're doing, you can help the railroad. That's the way all our land sales will be made. Except you—and a few others—won't have to worry about getting set up. Any more questions?"

"Yup, there is. How do we know the railroad won't overcharge us, say, for a plow, or lumber, or seed?"

Larry hid his disgust behind a smile. "Because

you won't buy directly from the railroad. We're going over to Overman's Store—right across the street. You'll buy from him. The railroad pays the bill, copy to you. Then you pay back, starting next year, as I explained to Mr. Whelan. Prices may be a little higher here, but only because of shipping charges. You'll not be cheated."

"Who gets the shipping charges?"

Larry's voice grew sharp. "The railroad, unless you want to pay sky-high, to freight 'em in by team and wagon. Is there anything wrong with that?"

Briggs' mouth snapped shut, but Whelan said, "Sounds fair to me."

"Good, any more questions?"

Briggs rose to his feet. "Yup, when do we get started? Day's just sliding away."

"Now."

Larry downed his coffee and rose, the two farmers with him. He walked out to the porch where the two families were gathered. Larry smiled at them, and then he strode across the porch to the steps. Briggs spoke to his son, behind him, "Luke, you come along. Time you learned how to buy for a farm."

"Goes for you, Jory," Whelan added.

Larry led the way across the dirt street to the general store. Overman had just opened, and had not even reached his cubicle of an office at the rear. He turned in the aisle as the troop entered.

He blinked, but covered his surprise with a gulp and a smile. "Are these the folks you told me would come, Larry?"

Larry introduced them, including the gangling adolescents. "They'll need everything, from nails and sugar to lumber."

"I've got everything but the lumber," Overman said.

"You've got that, too. Sitting in a boxcar on the track, right now."

Overman blinked, caught himself, and spoke hastily to the farmers. "Just look around a while, gents. I'll be right with you. Larry, there's something in the office you ought to see."

He led Larry to the cubicle, closed the door, and waved Larry to a straight chair with a sagging bottom, beside his battered desk, every pigeonhole of which was stuffed with papers. Light streamed in from a small window. Overman sat down, fingers drumming on the desk.

"What do you mean, I've got lumber?"

"Just that. The railroad's billed it to you on consignment, plus the shipping charge. You don't pay until you sell it, and they—" Larry jerked his thumb toward the outer room—"they'll buy it, today."

"With what?"

"Railroad money, Harry." Larry chuckled. "You still don't quite believe it, do you?"

"Want to—but it's hard."

"Give their bill to me. Take your usual, reasonable profit on the lumber. We pay you."

"And them?"

"Railroad business, but I'll tell you. And this is only for you, Harry, so don't get any hopes up in the saloon or saddleshop, or anything like that. The railroad's gambling on these two, and a few more will make it. So we're backing 'em for supplies, equipment, building—even teams that they need. But for nothing else. They give us a note for your bill."

Overman sighed, ran his fingers over his jowl, and bit his lip. His thick graying brows suddenly clamped down. "Suppose another store comes in—or several? Will you make the same deal with them?"

"No—and the deal with you will be off, too. If more stores come in, there'll be enough people to support them. And that's what I've been saying all along will happen to Olanthe. Right now, the railroad wants these two—and maybe three more to start the ball rolling. You happen to be here already, and that's your luck."

Overman made a gesture of assent. "I reckon I am lucky. Glad for the business, but it kinda bothers me."

"Why?"

"They're farmers, and you're going to bring more farmers. That means trouble with the cattle drives, maybe the end of 'em."

25

Larry brought his lips tight together, and he stood up, looking down at the troubled storekeeper. "That again! O.K., if you prefer the cowboys once a year, I'll make this deal with someone in Grayling. Say the word."

"Oh, no! I didn't say that. I'm just worried a little."

"Then do your worrying with Dick Poole and Ace Clemson. I'm too busy."

He left the office, and Overman followed him out slowly. Larry walked over to Briggs, who was examining a sack of dried beans on the counter.

"Buy what you want, Briggs. Overman will make an itemized bill for you, and one for Whalen. Bring 'em to my office across the street, and we'll make up the notes you two can sign to cover 'em."

"Lot to buy—and haul. And we ain't got no way."

"Overman has. He'll do it free. See you later at the office."

Larry went directly to the railroad station, where Ross Gentry served as postmaster. There was a thick envelope from the Chicago office for Larry.

Ross was worried about the solitary car on the siding. "When will they unload it? Cattle will be in before long, and I got stock cars coming. Take up every foot of that siding."

"It'll be gone long before," Larry assured him.

26

Back in his office, he opened the envelope. Marlowe's letter congratulated Larry on his first two sales, and enclosed a printer's proof of an advertisement.

"We're putting this in every paper in every farming state and county east of the Mississippi," Marlowe wrote. "And we've also made a poster of it for every railroad station and feed store. We're backing you here all we can. The rest will be up to you—and good luck."

Larry grunted, "And you also mean, I'd better make my luck."

He opened out the ad. Bold letters jumped at him: RICH KANSAS VIRGIN FARM LAND, CHEAP! Lines of close type followed, and then letters only slightly less bold at the bottom: APPLY LAND OFFICE C&FW RR, CHICAGO, OR DIRECTLY TO LAWRENCE CRANE, LAND OFFICE, OLANTHE, KANSAS. HURRY!

Slowly, Larry folded the ad, then gazed out the window, into the distance. He knew Briggs and Whelan were here in response to a trial advertisement in a small Indiana paper, but this ad . . . this meant that land buyers would come flocking, giving him a few short months to succeed or fail as a land agent.

Briggs and Whelan came in, and dropped the bills for their purchases on his desk. Larry had each man sign his own invoice, then pushed the bills into a pigeonhole, and reached for his hat.

"You'll want to see your land again. So we'll ride out. How about your wives and children?"

"Time enough for them to see it," Briggs answered.

"They'd just be in the way, right now."

Larry made no comment as he started to the door. Then he turned, and Briggs and Whelan drew up behind him. Larry pointed to a huge surveyor's map hanging on the wall just beyond. Two connecting red squares broke the map's white-and-black pattern.

"I told you once before, you've picked land that lies right across the cattle trails. I tried to tell you, in the next few months, the herds will hold up any farming you might plan. So, I'll still make an exchange for the land along Crow Creek, if you want it. No trouble there."

The two farmers exchanged a long, searching glance, and Whelan seemed indecisive, on the edge of accepting. But Briggs answered, "We chose the best farms. And you said the Texas cattle would stop coming."

"I said," Larry corrected, "eventually they will stop coming. I know that for a fact—but not this year, and maybe not next."

Whelan gently cleared his throat, but Briggs cut in, "Lot to do before we actually start plowing, or anything. Them cows won't keep us from building a house and barn and such things, will they?"

"Depends on where you want to build them."

"Let's go see." Briggs answered with such finality that Whelan didn't argue.

A short while later, Larry and the farmers drove from town in a buggy rented from Tatum, the livery man. The team looked overfat from lack of work, but stepped out eagerly, for all that. Circling the stock pens, Larry lined out southward over the prairie. The only roadway was a wide path trampled by the herds for the last five years. The town, with its pens and false fronts, disappeared in the distance behind them.

Some ten miles southward the ground become a series of wide, rolling swales. The buggy rolled down into them, and then rolled up, like a boat on a strange sea. At last, Larry saw a peeled pole with wind-beaten, white cloth still tied to it.

He reined in. "Corner marker between your farms. This is your north boundary. Which farm do we look over first?"

"Take his'n," Whelan said, and Larry slapped the reins, heading southeast. They left one cattle trail, but soon came on another, and then another. The trails were terminal arteries of the one main trail up from Texas, all ending at the Olanthe pens.

Beyond the third trail was a rise of land that might possibly be called a hill. It was crowned by five widely-spaced trees. Briggs pointed. "That's it. House there."

The three tramped about the hillcrest, as Briggs planned sites for his buildings, then they looked out over the grassy sea. They could not see the marks of the cattle trails. All three envisioned the conversion of the grass into plowed fields. Larry felt a lift of triumph.

Later, they rode to Whelan's section, and allocated building sites on a flat grassy area protected on the north and west by a wavering line of trees.

They returned to the buggy and, driving slowly back to the nearest trail so they could head north to Olanthe, Larry said, "Overman will bring tents with the rest of the stuff, tomorrow. It's a loan from the railroad."

"Tents?" Whelan asked.

"Big ones. We housed railroad workers in them when we were laying track. Big enough for your family. Soon as you know how much lumber you need for your houses, that'll be delivered."

"And billed," Briggs grunted.

Larry was unruffled. "That's right. We're helping farmers, not beggars."

Briggs subsided.

Long before they hit the cattle trail, they saw a lone rider coming up from the south. At first, he was only a dot against the sky, but, as rider and buggy converged, his shape became clear.

They came to the trail, and Larry reined in as the rider approached, presenting a leathery but young face, tanned by sun and wind. The high cheekbones lengthened the face. A wide-brimmed, high-crowned hat shaded his features.

Larry noted the faded kerchief about the strong neck, and the equally-faded blue shirt that strained at shoulders and chest. The rider wore a cartridge-studded gun-belt, a holstered Colt at his right thigh. He wore the scarred chaps of the Texas country, and high-heeled but comfortable boots, thrust into wide stirrups. His rifle nested in a scabbard on one side of the saddle, and a coiled lariat on the other. A blanket roll protruded behind the cantle of the saddle. He reined in a few feet away, and assumed an easy slouch.

"Howdee."

Larry lifted his whip by way of greeting, and asked, "Heading for Olanthe?"

"That's right. Riding ahead of the Flying W trailherd." Washed, sun-wrinkled, blue eyes scanned up-trail. "Any cattle come into Olanthe yet?"

"None."

Wide, crooked lips broke into a pleased smile. "Now, I figured Flying W would be first! I'm Brace Denbo, by the way. Trail boss of Flying W."

Larry introduced himself and companions. Denbo nodded gravely to each, his eyes sharp, and searching Briggs and Whelan. Larry asked, "How far back's your cattle?"

31

"Oh, maybe ten days, two weeks. I been pushing ahead pretty fast. Figure to get pens and beef buyers, so the stock will bring top, first-of-season price."

"Other herds behind yours?"

Denbo smiled crookedly. "Sure, strung clean down into Texas. Well, maybe we can ride together into town?"

Larry nodded, lifted the reins, and the buggy jerked forward. Denbo rode alongside, his broad back swaying easily in the saddle to the motion of his paint horse. Briggs and Whelan watched him, Briggs with narrowed eyes.

"Cowboy, huh?" he whispered, and Larry nodded. "Heard of 'em, but first time I ever saw one. How many head in a herd?"

"I don't know—several hundred, or a thousand, I hear."

"Lot of head," Briggs said and looked sideways at Whelan, who said nothing.

Denbo waited while the farmers got off the buggy at the hotel, and then he rode alongside Larry to the livery. He swung out of the saddle as Larry descended from the buggy. Denbo turned, the reins loose in his hand. His voice was friendly. "What do you do around here? First time I've seen you."

"Work for the railroad. Sell land."

"To them two?"

"To them—and anyone else."

32

"Mmmm." Denbo looked back to the hotel. "Farmers, ain't they? . . . Well, I sure hope they bought in the right location around here. Nothing like fences or plowed fields to rile up feelings."

"It's their land," Larry said.

"That's right. And my cattle. Friend, I'm no different than any other trail boss. My cows go to market, come hell and damnation. I'd feel mighty mean if a fence got in the way—and a plowed field? . . . it could get mighty torn-up."

He smiled pleasantly, and turned toward the stable, speaking over his shoulder. "Something for you and your friends to chew on."

# III

Larry was occupied with the Briggses and Whelans, so he did not become aware of the impact of Denbo's arrival till well on into that first night.

Larry had left Denbo at the livery stable, and gone to his office. He wrote Marlowe a brief letter, expressing his confidence in the ad, and took the letter to Ross at the station. He stopped off at the Texas Saloon. Marshal Ace Clemson was Bat's one customer when Larry entered and ordered his drink. For a while, the three men said nothing, after the usual greetings.

Ace broke the silence. "Your friends are settled?"

"They will be," Larry answered.

"Hope so. Brace Denbo said he run into the three of you, south of town."

"That's right."

Bat refilled the glasses around, signifying this drink was on him. He cleared his throat, and had a hard time wording the question. "Where they going to farm, Larry?"

"They won't turn a furrow, for months. When they do, it'll be down that way."

"Denbo figures they'll block the trail," Ace said softly.

"It bothers Denbo?" Larry flared.

"Not him—not any trail boss or crew. But it ought to bother your friends, if they got any idea about fencing off the trail."

"Who said they did?"

Ace studied Larry, who had turned in anger. The marshal calmly finished his drink, and rubbed his fingers over his moist lips. "No one said they did. But it figures, and anyone can see it—you, most of all."

Larry's eyes lost their angry glint. "In time— next year, the year after. You're right. But, by then, it won't matter."

"It'll matter to me and the whole town," Bat growled, behind the bar. "Without the Texas men, I might as well close up, and move off yonderly, and it's the same with every merchant in town."

"You'll have new customers," Larry insisted wearily. "I've told you that."

"Tell it to Denbo, then. He don't have any different plans for next year, or the year after, that I know."

"I might do that," Larry answered, and placed his empty glass on the bar.

That night, Denbo appeared in the hotel dining room. Seen in lamplight, he looked taller, and his rolling cowboy walk gave him an unintended air of over-assurance. Larry, sitting at a big table in the midst of the Briggses and Whelans, could only nod a reply to Denbo's faint smile of greeting. Briggs was taking up Larry's attention with one of his questions about the land deal.

Denbo took a seat alone at a table in a far corner, and watched Briggs, then Whelan, then Larry, with a smile of amusement.

Kathy placed a huge platter on the main table, and then went to Denbo's. Larry saw Denbo's tanned face light up in appreciation of Kathy's loveliness. Larry could not blame him for that, but he felt a catch of alarm at the way Kathy instinctively touched her golden hair, and smiled at Denbo.

"Seems to me," Briggs said, "you keep rolling up expenses for us. We're never going to get out of debt."

Larry's attention jerked back to Briggs. He realized how much he disliked this plump man of the furrows, his shrewd, narrowed eyes, his pursy lips.

"We can stop right here, Briggs. We'll cancel the land sale, tell Overman to forget the supplies, and you can catch the next train east, back to Indiana."

Briggs looked startled, then disappointed and half angry. Larry continued, his voice a shade milder, but still firm. "Once Overman makes delivery, there's no backing out. That'll be in the morning, unless I stop him."

"But—"

"And you'll pay your own fare home. How about it?"

Silence had fallen on the table, and Denbo's voice came clearly from across the room. ". . . a sight for sore eyes, Miss Kathy. You're remembered down in Texas, the whole year through."

"You're flattering me, Mr.—"

"Now, I never said I'd back out," Briggs drowned out the voices. "We come here, and we intend to stay. I just want to make sure everything's fair and square."

Larry kept his eyes on Kathy, who now turned away and walked back to the kitchen. He saw the pleased smile on her lips, and he threw Denbo a look. Denbo watched admiringly after Kathy.

"You can't blame a man for being careful," Briggs continued.

Larry's attention snapped back unwillingly, and he answered coldly, "No, I don't blame you for that. But you give me the feeling you don't trust the railroad, Overman, or me. None of us intends to rob you."

"Now, I didn't say—"

"And you haven't said if you're backing out, or going through with the contract, Briggs. I'll have to know now."

Briggs' round face reddened, and he sputtered as he looked about the table. Whelan, not looking up, paid close attention to a ball of bread his knobby fingers were forming. Jory stared open-mouthed, and Briggs' son Luke, sitting across the table, looked frightened. The girls were silent and round-eyed, sensing the tension. The two women sat still, eyes on their plates, shoulders set against a blow.

Larry met Briggs' angry, searching eyes. The farmer reddened even more, then his glance slid away. "No point in getting mad, Crane. I made a deal. I'll go through with it."

"Glad to know it. I'll see you folks in the morning, then."

Larry pushed back from the table, and rose as Kathy came in with Denbo's food. She paid no attention to Larry. He turned sharply, and went out on the porch. The western sky was bright with afterglow, and twilight was about to fall. Larry dropped into a chair. Why had he challenged Briggs so harshly? Denbo's smiling voice and Kathy's reaction—that, Larry confessed to himself, was the real cause of his anger at Briggs. Personal feelings, intruding in business, could cause him serious trouble someday.

Voices, within, grew in volume as the diners came out into the lobby. They faded up the stairs, and Larry eased back in his chair. Then Whelan came out on the porch. He stood at the top of the steps, making a show of looking up and down the street. He shoved his hands in his pockets, took them out, shoved them in again. He shifted his weight several times. Then, at last, he turned.

"Crane—about Obed."

"What about him?"

"Well . . ." Whelan moved the edge of his heavy shoe along a crack between two boards. "Maybe, it's not about Obed Briggs, but about me. I don't think like he does. I figure I've got a fair deal from you people, and a lot of help."

"Thanks for that."

"Obed's smart about money things, Mr. Crane. That's his way. He's honest, I guess, but he don't like to spend a penny more'n he has to—"

"But now," Larry put in, "he's forced to, if he wants to get established."

"That's right, but Obed don't like it. He's not one to give a favor, except to a close friend or neighbor, and so he don't understand why the railroad's helping him."

"We're not doing a favor. I explained."

"That's right, but Obed ain't worked it out for himself, yet. He figures that Crow Creek land had something wrong with it because you kept trying to sell it."

"Ridiculous!" Larry's voice sharpened. "But you turned it down, too."

Whelan looked away, and then shrugged. "There's just two of us going to start farming. Obed was set in his choice, and I didn't want to be without neighbors. That's just about it, Mr. Crane, for that Crow Creek land looked all right."

"I can understand that. My apologies."

"None needed, and none wanted. 'Night, Mr. Crane."

"Good night."

Whelan walked inside, and Larry settled in his chair again. A few moments later, Denbo came out, walking easily, a toothpick working in his mouth. He nodded to Larry, grinned, and jerked his thumb toward the dining room. "Quite a passel you herded in there."

"New to the country. I can't turn them loose, for a while."

"And you're new. I didn't see you last year."

"So you said, this afternoon."

Denbo took Whelan's place at the top of the steps. Larry considered the world of difference between the two men. Denbo's kind had brought the Texas cattle to railhead and market since the end of the Civil War. They had followed fur traders, explorers, and railroad builders. Now, maybe, Whelan's kind looked awkward, lost and uncertain, but their turn had to come.

Denbo intruded. "How long you figure on staying here?"

"Me—or the land office?"

Denbo looked up sharply from the cigarette he was expertly rolling. "Both."

"I could be gone tomorrow, if the railroad decided to transfer me. The office? . . . a long, long time."

Denbo twisted the end of the paper, put the

cigarette in his mouth, and struck a match. He looked through the flame a second, and then lit the cigarette. "Selling land—to anybody?"

"Anybody, if anybody fits in with the railroad's plans."

Denbo whipped out the match flame. "We never heard nothing like this, down in Texas. So you figure to fill up this range?"

"That's the idea."

Denbo looked through the open door of the hotel as though summoning up a vision. He worked his lips a while, and then said, "How about a drink? I ain't seen my friends since last year."

"Thanks, but I'd be a stranger, and you're meeting old friends. Another time."

"Another time."

Denbo descended the steps and walked down the street. Larry watched him till he disappeared into the Texas Saloon.

The next week proved a busy one for Larry. Overman delivered the tents and the other supplies. The tents up, and the two farm families established in their temporary homes, innumerable wagonloads of lumber arrived, under Larry's direction, at the two building sites.

Briggs complained only once, for he had heard about the typical sod house that homesteaders

41

built on government land. Larry agreed that such a half-cave, half-house would be cheaper.

"But, sooner or later, Briggs, you'd have to leave it. And you'd have to pay for the lumber in cold cash on the line. Now you don't. I want— or the railroad wants—to see two solidly built houses. We want to show 'em to other people looking for farms out here."

By late Saturday afternoon, Larry felt he had completed his first big job. He returned to his office in Olanthe, dropped into the chair before his desk with a sigh of relief, and glanced through the mail. He was too tired to be overexcited by half a dozen queries about farm land. Soon, he left the office and walked to the hotel.

Four well-dressed men occupied chairs on the porch. They were strangers to Larry but, obviously, not to the town. In the lobby, he met Kathy coming down the steps from the upper floor. She smiled, sighed wearily, and said, "We're beginning really to fill up. The season's starting."

"I can see. Who are the men on the porch?"

"Cattle buyers—from Chicago, Kansas City, and St. Louis. In a few more days, every room will be taken when the drovers come in." She brushed the hair from her temple. "I have to start supper. In a week, we'll be on two shifts for every meal."

Kathy hurried away to the kitchen.

After cleaning up, Larry came downstairs, sauntered out on the porch, saw the strangers still there, talking beef prices. He crossed the porch, and walked to the Texas Saloon.

The moment he turned the corner, he saw changes. Even the cheap hotel, which was sandwiched between the Texas Saloon and Dick Poole's gambling hall, was open. Larry heard the sounds of moving furniture, sweeping, and rough cursing as he mounted the steps of the Texas and pushed through the batwings.

Bat Owens stood in the center of the room, directing the cleaning of tables and the spreading of new sawdust on the floor. A new man checked stock behind the bar, and paused to fill Denbo's empty glass. Ross Gentry, looking tired and nervous, nursed his drink, and his sad eyes lighted when he saw Larry.

Denbo nodded as Larry came up and ordered. Ross spun a coin across the bar to pay for Larry's drink, and answered Larry's questioning look. "That's to say thanks for getting that boxcar out of the way. From now on, nothing but cattle cars on that switch track."

Larry lifted the glass in acknowledgment, and gestured with it to Denbo before he drank. Back of them, Bat cursed at a swamper as a heavy table scraped across the floor. Larry said, "The town's coming to life."

"Wait a few days," Ross answered. "It'll be hard

to sleep, day or night. Things get to roaring, and they never stop until the last steer heads east."

"And Flying W beef will pen and load first," Denbo added complacently. He turned to Larry. "I rode south today. Your friends are mighty busy."

"Building homes—and that takes them off my mind for a time. Buy you a drink?"

"Sure, and thanks. But whose mind do they get on now?"

Larry frowned while Denbo continued. "Like you said, both houses are off the trail, so they won't bother the herds coming in. Still, I wonder about a heap of things."

"Such as?"

"How come your railroad has land laying right across the trails? Seems like you could've picked just as good somewhere else."

"The railroad didn't pick. When we built the line across the country, the government helped us by giving open land to us. We had to take what was given, and we're glad to get it. It's that simple."

"But here in Olanthe," Denbo objected, "seems like you could have asked for another strip, somewhere."

Larry shook his head. "The grant was set by Congress, friend. We got alternate sections, checkerboarded on each side of the main line, from the edge of settlement to the Coast. That stretch south of here happened to be one of the sections. Nothing can be done."

Denbo considered his drink, frowning. "And you're going to sell to farmers and block us off?"

"We're forced to sell. The more people out here, the more freight and passengers. Without that, the railroad goes out of business."

Denbo pursed his lips, and his blue eyes shadowed. "By next year, then—"

"More settlers," Larry admitted. "It won't be long before you'll stop coming to Kansas, Denbo. Not because we'll block you, but because there are railroads to be built through Texas itself. You'll take short drives, then."

"I ain't heard of it—or my boss. All we know is we have to come here, or go out of business ourselves."

"It'll happen the way I say," Larry insisted. "Next year, the year after."

"Suppose it don't, and your sodbusting friends block us off from Olanthe?"

"Well . . . the trail can be rerouted west of here."

"Nothing west but prairie grass, friend. Nope, I figure to keep coming right here to Olanthe. But that's next year. Right now, I keep worrying about this year."

"No need to."

"Somehow, I figure I do. Today, I saw your friends up on a hill, building a house. Now, that's all right. But then, I could figure that, from up on that hill, they could see cattle—say my Flying W—coming, a long way off."

"They could. What about it?"

"Why, they'd have time to get down to the trail, and stop my beef. It's their land."

"Legally, I suppose they could," Larry admitted. "But I've warned them, the herds will come through, and to leave them alone."

Denbo smiled. "Now that's good to hear. Sort of helps a little. You see, my segundo, bringing the beef up to Olanthe, has a hair-trigger temper. Some say he's a mean jigger, and that may be, but he can handle cattle, and that's all I care about. Pardee Malan wouldn't like to be stopped. He wouldn't like it, at all."

"That sounds like a threat."

"Why, friend, you've got the wrong idea! I'm just telling you how Pardee is—and the way I am. Something you ought to know, and pass along to your friends on that hill. Now—have another drink?"

Larry hesitated for a second, and then he smiled. "This time, yes."

# IV

For two days, Larry watched the town fill up, and come to surprising life. The trains, east and west, all stopped now, and unloaded passengers. More cattle buyers registered at the hotel. Women descended from the coaches, sisters to those who had stayed on the year through, and swiftly disappeared into the houses.

The empty buildings along the row became throbbing hives of work, renovation, cleaning. Gamblers came. Faded signs on the high false fronts of the saloons became garish with new paint. Cattle cars, a solid line of them, filled the switch line before the pens, and Ross swore when a freight car, loaded with shipments for the merchants, was switched onto the track. Ross pressed them to unload, so the car could be moved out for the needed stock carriers.

The peaceful rhythm of the hotel began to change. Kathy and her mother, a tall, gray-haired replica of her daughter, were constantly in the kitchen or busy in the rooms. After supper, there was constant movement down the corridor, and men sat on the porch, cigars glowing in the darkness. Larry watched, fascinated.

Several times, he saw Denbo talking to buyers. The trail boss moved in and out of the hotel—to the pens, to the Texas Saloon where the buyers gathered each day and watched south for a sign of the first cattle coming in, then back to the hotel again.

Larry rode out to Briggs' place several times. Whelan and his son helped build the house on the hill, a cooperative effort that pleased Larry. The framework now stood bare against the prairie sky, looking deceptively lofty in this flat land of grass.

One night, Larry tried to catch Kathy's eye as she moved from table to table, but she had time only for a smile and a brief word. He gave up, glad to see that Denbo also had no chance to talk to her. Denbo left the dining room with him, but they parted in the lobby, Larry going up to his room.

Larry could not relax as he had hoped to do. Continual bootsteps in the hall, the steady murmur of voices on the porch below his window, movement along the dark street, and the glow of lights from all the stores added to the air of expectancy that pervaded the town. At last, Larry put on his shoes and tie, shrugged into his coat, and left the room.

He went to the Texas Saloon. He had a drink. He loafed at one of the tables. He listened to the talk at the bar, the bets on when the first herd would arrive, the speculations about prices and shipping. Men came and went. Finally, he left the saloon, and turned to walk along the street toward his hotel.

At the corner, he came on Ace Clemson standing in the shadows, light reflecting from his badge. The marshal turned sharply as Larry approached, slouched again when he saw who it was. "Evening, Crane."

"Evening, Ace. I've never seen you out so late."

"You will from now on—and later."

"Expecting trouble?"

The marshal smiled tightly. "Say I'm practicing for it. Might be, one of these buyers'll get a little drunk or noisy—or get in an argument over a card game or one of the girls. That's easy broke up. But when the cowboys come, my jail will be busy, and I reckon I'm about to earn my pay for the year, starting any day now."

The two men stood a few moments, looking at the lights along the row. Larry's eyes moved to the dark, vague shapes of the cattle cars, and the squatting shadow of the station. For the moment, there was no sound. Even a piano somewhere had stopped its tinny beating. Larry had the strange feeling that this peace was false.

"Well, it's quiet now. Time for bed."

"So it is, except for me. 'Night, Crane."

"Good night."

Larry had taken two steps when Ace called him back. "Have you ever worn a gun, Crane?"

"No."

"Can you handle one?"

"I was in the cavalry—four years through Virginia and Tennessee."

"Then you can. Wear a gun, Crane. You never know when some half-drunk puncher will get mad over nothing at all. They've been months on the trail, so they're wild and randy when they get turned loose. Better yet, stay off the streets at night as much as you can."

Larry stared, and Ace continued calmly. "I keep 'em here on the line. Any of 'em get on the main street without any business being there, get thrown in jail. But still . . . well, move and talk soft, Crane. 'Night."

Ace's cigarette made a glowing arc as he flipped it into the dust, and turned away. Larry watched his stolid silhouette grow small against the lights along the row.

Larry thoughtfully walked to the hotel, which was dark except for the glow of a low-trimmed lamp in the lobby.

He stepped up on the porch, and halted. A woman sat in one of the chairs. Kathy said wearily, "You're up late."

"Restless, but that's gone now." He moved to a chair beside her, and sat down. "But how about you?"

Her laugh came warm, out of the darkness. "I suppose I'm resting before I go to bed, if that makes sense."

"It does."

"Mother's sensible. She's been sound asleep for an hour, at least. I should go in myself. Dawn comes awfully soon."

"I won't keep you."

"That's all right. It's good to talk while you rest—about something more than cattle prices."

He said nothing, and they sat in silence for a time. Then she sighed again. "I wish the year's work could be spread evenly instead of coming all at once."

"I'm sure it will—soon."

He sensed her eyes studying him in the darkness. "Mr. Briggs and Mr. Whelan—you really believe in them—their kind, don't you?"

"Very much."

He heard the rustle of her dress as she shifted in her chair. "I wish I could, really. I wish I could believe that someday Olanthe will become more than an end-of-trail town. But I can't see anything else."

"Why not?"

"Just a feeling, I guess. No, something more. Harry Overman and Bat Owens and even your friend Ross Gentry don't think it will change."

"But Briggs and Whelan being here—"

"Let's see what it means. You don't know what cowboys can do when something gets in their way."

"I have an idea what they'd like to do—and

Olanthe, too, for that matter. There have been hinted threats."

"I'm sorry, truly. But it was bound to come. I guess we're afraid we'll lose out, all the way around. This would be a ghost town if the herds stopped coming. That's why Ace Clemson tries to let them go wild as wild and still keep them in line a little bit. He throws the worst in jail overnight, and lets him go the next day. If he didn't, they'd wreck the town. And we live on the money they bring. It's all we've got."

"I want to change that. I will."

"You believe it. I wish I could. But I know what can happen. Did you know Brace Denbo has been watching your farmers?"

"I know—and some of the half-threats came from him."

"Don't blame him, really. He's protecting his interests just as we all are."

Larry didn't reply for a while. At last, he said, "He's used to a way of life, like all of you."

"And he's really very nice."

Larry hesitated, and then blurted, "He's come every year, hasn't he?"

"And stays here. Mother and I both like him."

"I can see."

She said nothing for a moment, and then stood up abruptly. "Shouldn't I, Mr. Crane?"

He jumped to his feet, realizing his mistake. "Of course! It's just that I . . ."

He groped for a way to say it, but she asked, with a touch of asperity, "That you what, Mr. Crane?"

He couldn't check the words, "That I like you—very much—and I've noticed—" He came up short. "I hadn't meant to say that. It's none of my business, and I have no right . . . I'm sorry, but please understand."

The faint lamp-glow through the open door revealed her face, softened its lines, and made her even more beautiful. He saw her firm, angry jaw soften, and her lips move into a smile.

"No, you have no right—and I do understand. I'm glad you—good night, Mr. Crane."

She wheeled, and disappeared through the door, his "Good night," following after.

Troubled, he moved to the porch rail, and looked out on the dark street. Suddenly, he realized he had given her some faint idea of how he felt. And she had been pleased! He chuckled triumphantly, went to his room, and contentedly sought sleep.

Next day, Larry spent the whole morning answering mail queries about the railroad land. He sealed the envelopes, put them in his coat pocket, and strolled leisurely to the railroad station. He had just reached the platform when a shout and a flurry behind him made him turn.

He saw Denbo swing up on a horse behind a dusty cowboy. The cowboy spurred, and the horse bolted for the corner of the street, and turned up it toward the hotel. Larry watched the settling dust, then shrugged, and entered the station.

Ross took the letters. His expression was harried. "Flying W's just down the trail. A rider came in for Denbo. I hear there's three other herds, right behind them. They'll be fighting for pens and loading. Extra locomotives coming from east and west, and I sure hope they get here on schedule."

"I saw Denbo."

"His rider was sure lathering about something, but then, they always get proddy at the end of the trail."

Larry left the station. He had just stepped down from the platform when Denbo, now mounted on his own paint, spurred around the corner, and streaked toward the far end of the pens. His cowboy rider streaked after him. Larry frowned, watching the rolling dust clouds settle.

He walked back toward his office, and was about to enter when he saw Tatum standing outside his livery stable, looking south. Tatum saw Larry, nodded, and then looked south again. Larry called, "Expect the herds?"

"Maybe," Tatum called back across the street. "Flying W's held up south of here."

"What held 'em up?"

"Don't know. But Denbo and his rider were plain fighting-mad when they cut out of here."

Larry swallowed hard, a clutch of fear at his

throat. "Saddle me a horse—a fast one. I'll want it in five minutes."

He ran to Overman's store and blurted his order to the surprised proprietor who was waiting on a lady customer. "Colt! holster! cartridges and gunbelt! Fast, Harry!"

The customer stared at Larry with surprise as Overman hurried to a case, and pointed to a display of heavy revolvers. "Take your choice. All forty-fours. I'll get the rest."

Larry pulled weapons from the case, tested their balance and action, picked one, and turned when Overman hurried up with a new belt and holster and a box of cartridges. Larry snatched them from his hand, snapped the belt about his waist, buckled it, broke open the box, and thumbed shells into the Colt's chamber, then plunged the weapon into the holster.

"Bill the railroad. I'll settle when I get back."

Overman could only nod blankly to Larry's retreating back. Tatum had cinched a saddle on a rangy bay when Larry hurried into the stable.

Larry snatched the reins from Tatum's hands, led the horse outside, and swung into the saddle. A gouge of his heels set the bay off like an arrow down the street.

He circled the pens, and headed directly south. Feeling a horse beneath him and a gun on his hip brought back the old days in Virginia. He was a cavalryman again. He dropped his hand to the gun, and his fingers curled about the walnut handle. The weapon blurred up and lined down with a smoothness Larry thought he had forgotten.

He replaced the Colt, and his heels drummed more speed from the horse. The miles whipped behind him. In the distance he saw the dark frame of Briggs' house on the hill. He dropped into a swale, raced up the far slope, keeping to the beaten cattle trail.

He reined in, the horse's hind legs sliding and kicking up dust. It snorted, tossing its head, but Larry kept tight rein as he peered ahead.

He saw the herd now, a low, undulating, black mass. Then he saw the riders circling before the cattle, and four men afoot in their midst. Larry spoke quietly to the bay, which moved forward at a walk.

He saw one of the riders was Denbo. Two of the other half dozen riders held guns on the men afoot. Larry recognized Briggs, Whelan, and their two sons. He saw rifles on the ground at their feet.

As he came closer, he heard one of the riders swearing. "I got half a mind to either blow your brains out, or string you up!"

Larry pulled his Colt from its holster, and let it hang at his side as he closed the distance. Suddenly, one of the riders saw him, and yelled. Denbo and the swearing man jerked around.

Larry said quietly, "You'll do neither."

"The hell I won't!"

Larry's arm came up, and his Colt lined on the puncher. "Not before I know what's going on."

Denbo said sharply, "Pardee! Crane! No shooting! We'll have a stampede!"

# V

Larry didn't take his eyes off the small, dark puncher with the thin lips and square-trap jaw. The man's eyes glittered wickedly as he kept his gun lined on Briggs. His lips curled as his thumb lifted to the hammer, dogged it back with a deadly click.

"Now you just try something, and this jasper gets a hole through his chest."

"And you'll get the second," Larry answered coldly.

Briggs' round face turned pale, and the two boys trembled. Denbo's harsh voice tore at the instant of silence. "Pardee! Damn it! Put that gun up! And you, Gates. No shooting."

Larry spoke without looking away from the man called Pardee. "Briggs, if you want to live five minutes more, pick your rifle up by the muzzle. No other way. That goes for the rest of you. Move over toward the house, and let the cattle go by." He saw their hesitation. His voice crackled. "Move! Or take a bullet."

Denbo snapped, "Pardee! Gates! Put up your guns. We're moving through."

The tableau held a second, and then Briggs bent down and gingerly picked up a rifle by the muzzle. Whelan and the boys followed suit.

Pardee met Larry's steady eyes with a glittering malevolence, and then, with a gesture, rolled his Colt in his hand, and dropped it into its holster. The farmers moved past Larry, who still held his gun on Pardee.

"It's over, Crane. Leather your Colt."

"When your boys move out the cattle."

"Get 'em out! Roll 'em along!" Denbo snapped.

The riders neck-reined their horses and turned to the cattle, Pardee riding arrogantly to point position. He twisted in the saddle, lifted a long arm, and shrilled, "Getttalonggg! Hi!"

Larry and Denbo moved their horses out of the way of the slow-moving juggernaut. The brown, heavy beasts started by, and Larry holstered his gun. Denbo, sitting beside him, said from the corner of his mouth, "Your damn farmers! Tried to hold us up—dollar a head!"

"They'll not do it again. I promise you."

"So do I! Next time they'll be buried!"

Briggs and the others had moved to positions behind Larry, whose attention was now on the river of cattle that was passing before him. He had never seen a trail-herd before and the very size of it fascinated him. A puncher came by, slapping a coiled lariat against the leather wings of his chaps.

Denbo sat ramrod-straight, his chiseled face tight with anger. His eyes flicked from beast to beast as though making a private tally.

Suddenly a rifle cracked, and then a second. The shots blended in a single roar. Some steers tossed their heads and swung out of line, eyes wild. Denbo whipped around as the rifles fired again. The lunging steers broke formation, and raced off at a tangent. Others followed, and Larry, stunned, heard the punchers' angry shouts. Riders whipped by him to turn the racing steers, which were drawing more and more steers after them. Suddenly, the brown, living river of animals changed its course.

Larry's horse snorted and reared as a mad-eyed steer came charging straight toward it, a dozen or more plunging behind. Larry neck-reined the horse, and beat his heels into its side, but the bay needed no urging. It raced away.

Larry had a glimpse of Briggs and his son, rifles in their hands, staring in dismay as the sluggish, peaceful herd changed into a racing fury. Then Larry's horse swept him off, just ahead of the stampede.

Larry threw a look over his shoulder, angled the bay to the right, and begged it to greater speed. The horse cleared the edge of the surging brown river behind it, and the stampede swept on to one side. Larry drew rein. The horse fought bit-and-check, but Larry held it in. The last of the racing animals swept by, and a thick cloud of dust enveloped Larry.

The dust thinned, and his vision cleared. He

saw the two farmers and their sons standing in stunned surprise. Denbo was gone. The herd was thundering northeast, raising a cloud of angry yellow smoke against the sky.

Larry turned his horse, and rode up to the farmers. Round-eyed, they looked up at him, Briggs and his son still clutching their rifles.

Larry found his voice through shaking anger. "Drop those rifles!"

Briggs stared, hardly comprehending, and then his lips pursed angrily. "Damned, if I do!"

Larry's hand dropped to his holster, and Briggs stared into the muzzle of the Colt. Luke Briggs' face turned pale, and his throat made a choking noise.

"Briggs, drop it! and you, Luke!"

The farmer's pudgy fingers tightened on his weapon, and his face mirrored defiance. Suddenly, flame lanced from Larry's Colt, and Briggs flinched as the slug whined by his head.

"The next will be bull's-eye," Larry said, through set lips. "Drop the rifle—both of you!"

The two weapons thudded on the ground, and puffs of dust flew up. Larry held his gun on Briggs. "You stopped the herd. Why?"

Briggs swallowed, and then regained courage. He growled. "It was crossing my land—my farm."

"You knew herds would. I told you—before you signed the contract. I told you to leave 'em alone. Why didn't you?"

Briggs answered stubbornly. "I do as I please on my own farm."

"I see you try." Larry held his Colt steadily on Briggs, and flicked his eyes to Whelan. "Maybe you can make more sense and explain this to me."

Whelan's lined, gaunt face took on the expression of a boy caught in a misdemeanor. He looked at Briggs and son, and then up at Larry. "He—we decided cattle crossing our land ought to pay for the right."

"A dollar a head," Larry said shortly.

"That's right."

"Whose idea was it?"

Whelan fell silent, and Briggs snapped an answer. "Mine. And it's no more'n right."

Larry stared at him, eyes hard, and Briggs finally shifted his weight, and looked away. Larry said, "Jory, pick up those rifles. Take them to the tent."

Jory Whelan glanced at his father, who nodded, and the youth picked up the weapons. He turned, and trudged away toward the Briggs' tent behind the hill. Larry watched him go, then straightened, and holstered his Colt.

He folded his hands on the saddlehorn, and waited until he knew he had his anger under control. He met Briggs' defiant look straight on. "The next time you use any of those rifles for anything but hunting, I'm taking 'em away from you. That goes for you, Whelan."

"Now listen, Crane!" Briggs started.

Larry turned a blazing face to him, and Briggs flinched involuntarily. "You listen, Briggs! I wondered all along why, if you were so damn anxious to get to farming, you picked this land. You gave me a story about not liking Crow Creek, but that was a lie."

Luke Briggs took a half-step forward. "You can't say that—"

"I can, and I will. And you'd better listen, too—and remember. Briggs, you planned this, from the time I told you about the herds. Did you, Whelan?"

"I—well—no, not then, but—"

"Briggs talked you into it," Larry finished scornfully. He straightened. "You stampeded that herd, Briggs. If they have any losses, you'll pay for it—and out of your own pocket—and right away." His lips flattened grimly. "That's what Denbo and his men will expect, if they come back to collect. You'll pay it in cold cash, or with your hide."

Briggs lost some of his defiance, and his lips needed moistening. He looked beyond Larry, and his face went pale. Larry turned his head, and saw Denbo riding up fast. Larry said swiftly, "Let me handle this—if I can. You'd better hope so, Briggs."

He reined his horse about, and cut between Denbo and the farmers. Denbo tried to angle about him, but Larry blocked him. Denbo reined in, and his right hand dropped to his holster. Larry kept both his hands in sight, holding the reins and resting them on the saddlehorn.

"Crane, get out of my way. I got a lesson to teach."

"The lesson's coming to them, Denbo, right enough. But I've already taught it."

"They need bullets."

"You're mad, and I don't blame you. How about the cattle?"

"Stampede's stopped."

"Lose any?"

"Just by luck, no. But Lord knows how many pounds they run off because those jaspers—"

"They're heading for the pens—and a quick sale," Larry cut in.

Denbo eased down in the saddle, still angry, but moving his hand from his holster. "I reckon you could say that. But—"

"I had their rifles taken away, Denbo. I read the riot act while they looked down a gun muzzle—mine. This won't happen again. I told them how it would be when you Texas men came through, but they didn't believe it. I think you've taught them they're lucky to be alive."

Denbo took a slow, deep breath. Larry asked quickly, "Sure there was no damage?"

"No more'n I told you."

"Would drinks around, back at town tonight, straighten things up?"

Denbo studied him, then looked beyond at the four men. His face tightened again, but he said softly, "I was mad enough to kill them. Thanks for stopping me, Crane. But I figure they got something coming, direct from me."

He lifted the reins, watching Larry expectantly. Larry tensed, and then eased back in the saddle, and turned his horse, moving beside Denbo to the four silent, scared figures.

Denbo studied them carefully, one by one, his eyes contemptuous. He thumbed his hat back from his forehead, and spoke to Briggs, principally.

"You could be dead—every one of you—with a bullet, or under the stampede. You deserve it." Carefully, he eyed each silent figure. "Flying W's run your blockade, but down yonderly—" The four followed the sweep of his arm—"down south, more Texas herds are coming. Somehow, I hope you try to stop one of 'em, for I'd sure love to put flowers on your graves."

On each of the four, in turn, he concentrated a hard, penetrating gaze. Then he straightened, and lifted the reins. "All right, Crane, if these jaspers got the lesson through their thick sodbusting skulls, I reckon I'll take that drink—me and the boys."

He turned his horse, and Larry, with a final

warning look, said, "I'll be back tomorrow," then turned his bay in beside Denbo. Some distance off, Larry looked back. Four figures were filing slowly toward their tent on the hill. Larry caught the red shimmer of a woman's dress, and his anger at Briggs flared again.

Larry straightened, and Denbo, slanting a look at him, said, "Maybe you've learned a lesson, too."

"How?"

"Them back there. This ain't farming range, and they don't belong."

Larry sighed. "Right now, I don't have much room for argument."

"So you see it, huh?"

"No. I just see one damn fool back there, but he doesn't change the picture."

"Stubborn, ain't you?"

"I've been accused of it."

Once again, Denbo thumbed back his hat-brim. He grunted, "Crane, I kind of like you. But you know what? You and me could get in one hell of a fight."

# VI

Several miles up the trail, they came on the tail end of the Flying W herd, moving again in a steady, brown flow. The drag man looked at them over the top of his bandanna, tied across nose and mouth to filter the dust.

Denbo called, "They're not spooking?"

The rider shook his head, and Denbo rode on up the line of cattle, searching among them with concern. He and Larry passed more riders—flankers, who had no need of the bandanna filter, and swing men. At the head of the herd, one huge steer, with gory, old scars on its flanks and shoulders, led the way several yards behind a slouched rider, who proved to be Pardee Malan.

Pardee looked around as Denbo and Larry drew up, and tensed in the saddle, though he didn't slow his pace. His black eyes flamed at Larry, then narrowed. Then he looked at Denbo. "Seems to me you'd have enough of that jasper. Those were his friends back there."

"Ease off, Pardee. We've lost nothing. Fact is, we're a couple of miles ahead, the way this beef run. He's buying drinks around, to beg our pardons."

Malan grunted, and looked ahead. "Sure there ain't some more blockades ahead?"

Larry answered quickly. "None—and there shouldn't have been, back there. It won't happen again."

Malan gave him a slashing look, then shrugged. Larry flushed, and Denbo moved in close beside him. "Pardee can lead these cows in. Let's ride ahead."

Larry moved out ahead with the trail boss, and they soon outdistanced the herd. Denbo slowed a bit. "Pardee will be all right. He has to let his temper have time to simmer down. Always was that way—quick to flare, and slow to get his feathers smooth again. But he holds no grudges. And you did throw a gun on him."

Larry's eyes flashed, and then he grinned apologetically. "That's right. But—"

"You did right, Crane. Not that I mind that sodbuster taking a bullet in the arm or leg, but I sure minded my herd skallyhooting over the landscape."

"Well, they did that, too."

"Not your fault." Denbo pointed ahead, and Larry saw Olanthe on the horizon. Denbo asked, "Who do I see about buying land?"

Larry swivelled about in surprise. "You? What for?"

"Anything wrong with me?" Denbo demanded, but before Larry could answer, he continued, "Anyone can buy it, can't they?"

"Anyone the railroad approves. But—"

"Thought so—so who do I see about it?"

"Why—me, or the C&FW Land Office in Chicago. Man named Marlowe. He's my boss."

Denbo nodded. "Something to know."

He would say no more. Soon they came to the long line of pens and cattle cars on the switch line. Denbo looked back at the dust cloud in the distance.

He straightened. "Tell you what, Crane. That drink for me and my boys—tonight, after supper. Me, I have to find a beef buyer, see that Flying W is penned and sold. Tomorrow we'll start loading, but that's tomorrow. All of us will be mighty busy when the herd gets in. So, meet you at the hotel, and together we'll meet the crew at the Texas. O.K.?"

Larry nodded, smiling. Denbo lifted his hand in a half-friendly gesture, and spurred ahead down the line of stock pens. Larry watched after him until he turned the far end of the pens and disappeared.

Larry rode slowly on. He turned the far end of the pens, and his horse gingerly stepped across the high rails of the switch, and then the main line. Larry glanced toward the station, and saw Denbo's horse standing at the edge of the platform, reins thrown over its head and dangling to earth—"ground-hitched," as they called it in this country. Denbo came out, and grabbed up the reins, swung into the saddle, and rode swiftly toward the line of buildings fronting the tracks.

Larry turned his horse to the station. A few moments later, he stepped inside, and found Ross in the telegraph office. "Denbo was in here."

"Yup. Sent a telegram down to Texas."

"About the herd arriving?"

Ross pulled at his mustache, and looked dismally sad. "Now, Larry, that's confidential, even if it was no more'n 'Good morning.' I got no call to speak about any man's business that he puts in a telegram."

Larry flushed. "Sorry, Ross. I'm in the wrong. I guess I'm just too curious."

"No harm done. And I wish I could answer you."

"Of course, you can't! Forget I asked. While I'm here, anything for me?"

"Nope, and I better get out to them pens. Flying W is due any minute."

He went out with Larry, and they parted on the platform. Larry rode to the platform, turned the bay horse in to Tatum, and paid for it. Tatum suggested the bay would be available any time, for a small fee. "Horses get scarce about this time of year, what with buyers wanting to ride out to meet the herds."

Larry made the deal, and then walked wearily across the street to the hotel. The porch and lobby were empty. He had not reached the stairs when a rear door was flung open, and Kathy appeared.

Her face fell when she saw Larry. "Oh, I thought it was someone wanted a room."

"That's me. I'm tired."

Her eyes fastened on his belt and gun. "When did you start wearing that?"

"Today."

"There's been trouble!"

His face softened, and he shook his head. "No trouble. But Ace Clemson suggested I wear one while the Texas men are in town. It's expected, I hear, like boots instead of shoes."

She searched his face. Slowly, relief replaced her concern. "Any word of the herds?"

"Flying W coming in, and I hear there's two or three right behind."

"Oh, dear! We'll be swamped!" She turned, and threw open the door. "Mother! Mother! We'll have to set more places at the table! More potatoes—!"

The closing door cut off her voice. Larry turned toward his room.

When he came down for supper, he saw many more places taken at the tables. Most of the newcomers appeared to be the usual beef buyers, but others he could not quite define, perhaps drummers. Denbo and Pardee Malan were sitting at one of the tables, and Denbo nodded to him across the room.

Larry sat down, and Kathy came up. After taking his order, she said, "The last time you have

71

a choice. Starting tomorrow, we go country-style. It gets too much having to take each order during the rush season."

She gave him a rushed, weary smile, hurried back to the kitchen, and brought his food. While he was eating, he saw Kathy go to Denbo's table, talk to the two men, and hurry off. Pardee Malan turned to watch her move, and something in his expression angered Larry. Pardee carried a half-grin on his thin, crooked lips, and his eyes were hungry. He turned to Denbo, nudged his elbow, and said something. Denbo looked steadily at him, said a word, and went back to eating.

Larry watched the swift change in Pardee's expression. His crooked grin vanished, and his lips twisted. Pardee revealed, in that split second, something ugly between him and Denbo.

After the meal, Denbo came over to Larry's table. "I got a buyer, but he dickered too long to load the beef on the cars tonight. They're in the pens, so my crew will be free for that drink you promised around."

"Name the time."

"Say an hour—I'll have the boys rounded up by then."

"An hour."

Denbo turned. Behind him stood Malan, working a toothpick in his mouth. He watched Larry with no expression, and did not bother to return Larry's nod. He turned on his heel, and strolled out behind his boss.

An hour later, through a flood of light from all the buildings on the street, Larry made his way to the Texas Saloon. Punchers stood at the bar, played poker at the tables, moved in and out of the batwings. Bat and his assistant worked unceasingly behind the bar.

Three women moved about the tables, stopping here and there as men hailed them. They took orders for drinks, and joked intimately with the men. They wore velvet gowns that showed wear to a sharp eye. The necks of the gowns were cut low.

Denbo stood at the bar, amidst a group of punchers. Malan, holding a glass, was studying the progress of one of the women about the room.

Denbo's tanned face warmed to a smile when he saw Larry, and he spoke loudly to the men about him. "Here's the jasper who's standing drinks. Crane, meet all but two of the Flying W crew. They're thirsty."

Larry smiled, and signaled Bat to serve around. Denbo made way as Larry pushed to the bar, and the Flying W men pressed close. Looking into the bar mirror, Larry saw Malan standing two places to his left. Malan met Larry's eyes with no sign of recognition. Bat Owens placed Larry's drink before him.

Larry paid. "You've added something, Bat."

"The girls? Every year. Makes the boys buy more whisky, and they tone up the place."

"Sure do!" the cowboy beside Larry said. "A sight to see. Reckon I'll get acquainted with one of 'em."

"Not now, you won't, Cowboy. They're working for me."

Bat hurried on, and the puncher sighed. Larry watched the mirror, and when the glasses were almost empty, he signaled Bat for another round, excluding himself. Denbo turned in surprise. "No need for that, Crane. The first round paid the debt."

"Say this is a bonus. I thought your herd was the only one came in."

"Only one in the pens now, but there's three more bedded down, couple of miles out. Trail bosses let some of the crews come in, turn about. There's Rafter H and Double Bar and Hashknife, and more coming. Give a few days, a week, and you won't move without bumping into a Texan, friend."

Larry shook his head in amazement, and Denbo bent toward him, over the noise. "You go watch the Flying W load the cars tomorrow, and see how the pens fill up with the other herds. Beef on the hoof, at several dollars a head. That's the crop we raise in Texas, and if it don't sell quick and for a good price, Flying W's in trouble. So are the others. And Olanthe's the nearest place we can sell. Maybe your sodbuster friends better stay a night in town, and see how it is."

"They won't bother you no—"

"Wish I could be sure of it. Maybe not me again, but some other brand. Either way, there's trouble. And you, friend, tomorrow night I buy you a drink."

"Why?"

"So you can get the idea, too—more'n you got it now. It might change some of them plans of yours."

Denbo lifted his empty glass as a sign of thanks, turned, and named two men to spell those back at the Flying W camp. The two grumbled, finished their drinks, and ambled toward the batwings.

Denbo turned back to Larry. "See you at the hotel, in the morning. Right now, I'm checking the pens. Pardee, see the boys don't get in trouble. Head 'em back to the camp, and then you turn in at the hotel."

Malan nodded, and Denbo walked away, through the batwings. Then Malan set his eyes on Larry's waist. "Where's your hardware?"

"What? . . . Oh, the Colt. I left it at the hotel."

"It'd pay you to wear it."

"That's what the marshal told me, while the punchers are in town."

Malan's lips moved in a tight smile. "That ain't exactly the reason for me. This afternoon, you were pretty handy with a gun. 'Course, I wasn't

75

looking. And I wonder if you really are that handy. Might be I could find a reason to find out. Oh, and thanks for the drinks. You got off cheap, didn't you?"

"So did you. Thank Denbo for it."

Both men leaned at ease against the bar, but their eyes were hard and their faces tight. Outside the rim of tension between them, the rest of the room faded into a blur of voices and clinking glasses. But only for a moment. Then a puncher, gay and unheeding, intruded.

"Hey, Pard! How about us seeing more of the town!"

Malan straightened, and pushed from the bar. Mockingly, he touched a finger to his hatbrim, and smiled at Larry. "I'll see you again—that's for sure."

He moved off with the Flying W crew, and the batwings rippled behind them.

# VII

Next morning, the dining room was even more crowded, not only with the usual buyers but also with men of Denbo's stamp—trail bosses of the other herds, with their segundos. Voices held to a low murmur as the men ate; much had to be done in a very short period of time.

Larry had a chance to nod to Kathy as she and her mother brought in huge platters of eggs, ham, and potatoes, and big, granite coffee pots, one to each table. The small tables had been pushed together to form three long ones, extending the length of the room.

Falling in with the mood about him, Larry quickly finished eating, gulped a cup of coffee, and pushed from the table. As he stood up, Malan appeared in the doorway to the lobby. He had an air of assurance and power. As Malan stepped into the room, Kathy removed an empty coffee pot from one of the tables. Malan watched her with his irritating smile. Kathy smiled at him, and Malan said something Larry could not catch. But he saw Kathy's smile freeze up, and an iciness come into her eyes. She stepped around Malan to the kitchen, her shoulders back, and her head high.

Larry moved toward Malan, but Malan didn't

see him. Malan pulled out a chair at the end of a table, and sat down, reaching for a platter of meat. Larry halted, choking down his anger. Then he turned on his heel, and strode from the room.

Larry went to Tatum's, saddled the bay, and rode toward the railroad station. As he neared the corner of the street, he heard a strange rumbling, mingled with human yells and the lowing of cattle. From the pens, punchers were driving cattle up wooden ramps and into the cattle cars. A pillar of dust rose into the clear sky. At the head of the string of cars stood a locomotive, smoke curling lazily from its funnel.

Ross came hurrying from the stock pens as Larry dismounted at the end of the station platform. Ross gave Larry a harassed look and said, "Some mail for you. And a wire. You're sure playing hob with things."

"Me?"

Larry followed Ross into the station office, and Ross spoke angrily over his shoulder, "I gotta figure some way to keep loading cattle, and still have room for a private car. I don't know yet how in hell I can do it but—"

"What's a private car to do with me?"

Ross snatched a yellow flimsy, and passed it to him. "There! And I got my orders from the Division Super. Just like that! I'm to arrange things!"

He shoved a bundle of mail at Larry. "This is

for you. Now get out, and let me go crazy in my own way."

He practically shoved Larry out of the office, after snatching up a pad of lading forms. He raced toward the stock pens, leaving Larry on the platform, reading the flimsy. It's message was short:

"Inspecting land development projects and progress. Will be in Olanthe Wednesday. Want to meet you and have report of Olanthe area then."

Larry whistled when he saw the signature of Jepson Reeves, a vice president of the railroad and top boss of the land office. Larry thoughtfully folded the paper. Why should Reeves come here, and why should he want to meet Larry and have a report? Larry shook his head, then shrugged. He gathered up the reins, swung into the saddle, neck-reined the bay around, and headed south.

Within a mile, he came upon the first herd awaiting its turn to the stock pens. The trail crew allowed the cattle a wide grazing ground, and Larry could not estimate the number of head in the herd. Curious cowboys, saddle-lazing on the herd's periphery, watched him pass. He waved a reply to their salutes, and rode on.

Farther on, he came on another grazing herd. Off to the west, a third herd was grazing. He began to understand why Ross was so distracted. Now he saw the skeletal framework of Briggs' house on the hill. Silhouetted figures were moving about. Soon he saw the brown tent at the base of the hill. Mrs. Briggs and her daughters were bending over wash tubs.

Up on the roof, Briggs and Whelan were setting the rafters as the long boards were passed up by Luke and Jory. Whelan saw Larry approaching, and stood erect, atop the framework. Luke came walking down the hill to meet Larry.

Luke stood with powerful legs apart, his attitude defiant. As Larry drew rein, the boy spoke a reluctant, "How-do."

Larry dismounted, pulled the reins over the horse's head, and let them drop. He answered pleasantly, "Hello, Luke. I came out to see your father and Mr. Whelan."

"Up there." The boy jerked his thumb over his shoulder. He was a blurred copy of his father; even his lips had a stubborn purse as he struggled for words, and finally blurted, "We don't care much about seeing you! There was no call for you to treat my Paw the way you did—and before everybody."

Larry studied the youth with understanding. "Your father could have been killed. Those cowboys were mad—and they had a right to be. Stampeding a herd was a foolish thing to do."

Luke glared; but Larry saw uncertainty in his eyes, and said, "And you could be dead right now, yourself."

Luke stopped glaring, then flushed, and turned

away, striding ahead of Larry up the hill. Briggs and Whelan had come down off the framework, and Briggs met Larry angrily.

"How many cows are going to cross my land without me doing anything about it? Look out there! And more coming!"

He pointed first to the grazing herd to the north, and then southward where another dust column rose to the sky.

"As many as come up from Texas," Larry answered evenly.

"How can I farm!"

"You have a house to build first. As for clearing land, you own plenty, away from the cattle trails."

"I'm supposed to kowtow to punchers on my own farm, am I? Maybe like you did with that Denbo, when you rode off with him?"

"I didn't kowtow. I told him you didn't understand about the trails—and that was lying for you."

Larry looked from Briggs to Whelan. "If I hadn't made peace for you, they could easily come back and settle a score they'd think you owe them—and you would, Briggs. What you did was the same as tearing up a man's plowed-and-planted field."

Briggs shoved his hands into his overall pockets, and glowered at the ground. "It's still my land."

"Briggs, no one denies that. But you knew what the conditions are here, and will be for a time. I came out to make sure you don't get any more wild ideas. The next time you hold up or stampede a herd, the trail crew might kill you. If they don't, I can promise you I'll bring the Olanthe lawman out here, and you'll spend a time in jail."

Larry gave them time for the threat to sink home, and then he spoke in a more friendly tone. "But I also came out to tell you I'm doing everything to bring in farm neighbors. It'll be then like it was back in Indiana, and Olanthe could become a county seat. Next year will be better, and the year after, better yet. You'll be able to fence-and-farm all you want. I doubt if there'll be any more herds."

"What makes you say that?" Briggs demanded. "Don't look like it to me."

"I happen to know railroads will be building into Texas. So why should the ranches drive cattle all the way up here when markets will be right at their doors down there?"

Whelan scratched his head, looked aslant at Briggs and back at Larry. "Makes sense, if it happens. Reckon all we can do is wait and see if it does."

"Fair enough. With that settled, is there anything you need from Overman or from the railroad? I'll be heading back to town."

The men exchanged glances, and Whelan shook

his head. "Nothing yet. Anyhow, we're used to hitching up for town if we need something. But thanks."

When Larry got within sight of the pens, he was surprised to find them almost empty, and the string of cars filled with cattle. Pardee Malan was ordering the final loading, and Denbo was talking intently with a cattle buyer who held a sheaf of papers.

Larry rode on into the town, stabled his horse, and went to the hotel. In the upper hallway, he came on Kathy coming out of a room she had finished cleaning. She smiled, but Larry frowned and said, "You look much too tired."

"I always seem to, the first few days of the season, and then I get used to it. By next week, I'll take it all in my stride."

"I hope so. At least, by tomorrow, or the next day, you'll have less work. Flying W is just finishing loading, so they'll be gone."

Kathy shook her head. "Not at all. End-of-trail is a vacation for them. The men are paid, and after weeks and weeks on the trail, they blow off steam. It'll be two weeks, a month, before they head back."

His eyes softened as he realized she had weary lines about her mouth and eyes. "Seeing you like this, I'm all the more sure things have to change."

Her face lighted with a smile. "Thank you, but I think the herds will always be coming."

She went to the next room, and disappeared inside. Larry went to his room, stripped off his coat and tie, and dropped on the bed. He looked out at the clear, peaceful sky, and listened to the sounds of the town. From the distance came the clanging of a locomotive bell, then the long blast of a whistle, followed by the clanking of metal. The string of cattle cars was moving across the switch to the main line, on its way east. The last sound slowly faded, and Larry eased back into his thoughts.

His thoughts broke off at the sound of boots in the hall. The boots passed his door, and stopped. Denbo had come in.

Larry glanced at his watch, and pulled himself from the bed—Time to do some office work before supper. He washed his face and hands, fixed his tie, and put on his coat. He opened the door, then remembered the letters he had left on the dresser. As he gathered them up, he heard someone coming up the stairway from the lobby. At the same time, a door opened near the head of the stairs. Larry stuffed the letters into his coat pocket, and stepped into the hall. He stopped short.

At the end of the hall, Pardee Malan stood facing Kathy. She was holding a broom and dustpan, and started to move around Malan. He took a step to bar her.

Malan said softly, "You and me ain't had a chance to get acquainted."

She answered lightly, "We're acquainted all we need to be for business, Mr. Malan."

She stepped forward. Malan put out his arm, barring her way. Malan smiled widely. "Now, that's not enough. Woman pretty as you takes the eye and—"

"Please, Mr. Malan. I don't care for that kind of talk."

"Don't you, now! Well, you get to know me better and—"

"Maybe she doesn't want to know you better, Malan."

Malan spun round to face Larry, two feet away. Malan's jaw dropped with surprise, and Larry spoke quickly to Kathy. "You can leave now. He won't bother you."

Gripping her broom and dustpan, Kathy went quickly round the two men and down the stairs. Malan and Larry faced each other. Malan found his voice. "You're getting to be a damn nuisance, Crane."

A shift of Malan's weight and a drop of his shoulder gave Larry a split-second warning. Malan swung for his jaw, and Larry jerked his head aside. Malan's blow raked his cheek, driving Larry back against the wall. Malan lunged, aiming another blow, but Larry blocked it, and threw a punch that landed on Malan's ear.

The cowboy staggered, his spur catching in the hall carpet, throwing him back, his arms flailing for balance. Regaining his balance, he dropped into a crouch, and his hand streaked to his holster.

A roar came from down the corridor. "Pardee! Hold it! Freeze."

Both men swivelled. Denbo stood in the hallway before his open door, light casting a golden glow around his powerful figure.

Pardee Malan dropped his hand from his gun, straightened, flung an oath at Larry, and said to Denbo, "This jasper keeps getting—"

"Shut up!" Denbo snapped. Malan's eyes flew wide and round as Denbo came and stood looking down at him. "I heard most of it—you and Miss Kathy. I told you twice already she's a lady, and leave her alone. Crane did right."

"But—"

"Pack your roll, and leave the hotel, Pard. Go down by the tracks with the rest of the crew, and stay there until we head back to Texas."

Malan's eyes blazed, and his lips worked a while before words burst out. "You can't do this. I've put up here and—"

"Pack, and git! Now! Or I'll pay you off, and you can get back to Texas however you can. You might have to do that, anyhow."

Pardee Malan eased back on his heels and, with the barest nod of acquiescence, moved around Denbo. He shot a look at Larry, and strode down the hall into his own room, slamming the door behind him.

Denbo took a deep breath, and exhaled it with a "Whoosh!", then turned to Larry. "Glad you stopped him. If you can wait until I'm sure he's left the hotel, I'll buy you a drink."

"Thanks, but I have to get to my office."

"Then, after supper."

Larry nodded and, after smoothing his coat and hair, walked downstairs, Denbo following him. When Larry entered the lobby, Kathy stood fearfully at the counter.

She gave Larry a sweeping glance, then smiled with relief.

"I—want to thank you."

"It's all right. He won't bother you again."

"Indeed, he won't," Denbo cut in. "You can rent his room. I ordered him to move."

"Oh? . . . Well, I guess that's best. And thank you, Mr. Denbo."

She smiled, turned, and disappeared through a doorway behind the counter. Larry started to turn, but stopped when he caught Denbo's lingering expression, his hard face and eyes gone utterly soft and warm. It shocked Larry to know Denbo felt as he did about Kathy Blaine.

# VIII

By supper time, Pardee Malan had left the hotel, and Larry was glad to know he was gone. Then time, with its exciting changes, made a blurred memory of the Malan incident.

The next day's mail brought a dozen inquiries about land, and two correspondents announced they were coming in person to Olanthe to look over the prospects for farming. Larry felt a glow of satisfaction.

As Kathy had predicted, the shipping-east of a herd did not signal its crew's return to Texas. Months of accumulated pay made cowboy pockets heavy, and there were too many tempting ways to lighten the burden. Larry found it practically impossible to get an evening drink at the Texas Saloon, which bulged with Texas men intent on drinking up Kansas.

Even Denbo got swept up into the exciting rhythm. For two whole days, Denbo would absent himself from the dining room, then he would show up looking more than a little haggard, and disappear again. Trail crews and beef came up from the south in a never-ending flood.

Station master Ross Gentry showed the period's wear-and-tear. Lines of weariness etched into his long face, and dark rims grew around his mournful eyes.

On a Tuesday, when Larry called for his mail, Ross passed his hand slowly over his face, gave a tremendous yawn, shook off fatigue, and passed a flimsy to Larry. "From the Division Super—to me, but something for you to know."

Larry scanned the paper, Ross clarifying the dispatcher's abbreviated jargon. "Reeves' private car will come in with a train of empties tonight. I'll spot it at the far end of the switch beyond the pens. Just a little less noise there to keep him awake. Why in hell does a vice president have to come this time of year?"

"To see me—and I'd like to know the why of that!"

"Well," Ross said, yawning, "you've got your problems, and I have mine."

Early the next morning, an ornate private car sat on the siding. It created a sensation in Olanthe, whose citizens were dull-eyed from the glimpse of cattle cars. Now, in their backyard, stood a splendor of varnished wood, stained glass, polished brass handrails, and shining back steps—something they had seen only as a steelpoint illustration in a newspaper.

Larry paused at the corner of the station. Looking at the car, he instinctively smoothed his string tie down the front of his shirt, and then tugged his coat evenly down around his shoulders. He made sure of his trousers' correct crease, and nodded at the sunlight on the toes of his boots. Then he grinned, and stepped over the main-line rails, and approached the rear car.

Placing his hands on the polished brass railing, he climbed the steps to the canopied platform. He lifted his fist to knock on the door, but thought better of it. He smoothed his coat, and tapped lightly on the window's varnished-wood frame. He had hardly time to lower his hand before the door opened. A pallid young man peered at him through rimless pince-nez. "Yes? What is your business?"

"Lawrence Crane. Mr. Reeves wants to see me."

The young man looked Larry over, his eye dwelling on the heavy buckle and the looped cartridges showing on Larry's belt.

A voice boomed from the darkness of the car. "Blogget, is that Crane?"

Blogget turned. "Yes, Mr. Reeves."

"Well, bring him in! There's work to be done."

"Yes, Mr. Reeves."

Blogget essayed a smile that was a pale, bloodless failure. "Come in, Mr. Crane. Mr. Reeves will see you."

Larry said "Thanks," and stepped inside. Blogget closed the door, then led the way, like a dark, thin ghost, along the corridor. Blogget stopped before an open door, and tapped respectfully, then his head momentarily disappeared within. "Mr. Crane, sir."

Blogget stepped back, extending his hand in a courteous gesture. Larry, hat in hand, stepped inside—a city office, whisked by magic here to the plains of Kansas . . . with a pigeonhole desk against the paneled wall . . . two upholstered chairs . . . and window drapes tastefully drawn to reveal not too much of Olanthe's rash of saloons.

Jepson Reeves was a small, fleshy man, round of face and stomach. He wore a dark cutaway coat, wing collar, and silken, navy-blue cravat aglitter with a jeweled pin. He had short legs and small feet. Bright light from the window behind made him appear in silhouette—a small man grandly filling a big job.

"Mr. Crane? Glad you could come."

The voice had a boom out of all proportion to the man's size. Larry, accepting the proffered hand, was instantly aware of power beneath the dimpled fingers.

Reeves waved Larry to one of the chairs and, as he turned, Larry saw his piercing, steel-blue eyes. Larry sat down, and Reeves moved with surprising, cat-like step to a small bar in the corner. "A drink, Mr. Crane?"

"Thanks, but not yet, sir."

"When?"

"Say, after sundown if the evening promises to be quiet."

Reeves returned empty-handed to his chair. He dropped into it, and knifed his blue eyes into Larry. " 'Quiet evening' you say—I hear you've raised some hell with some people around here."

"That's right, sir."

Reeves waited a moment, and then asked, "No explanation? Surely somebody was to blame."

"Not really, sir, by their own lights. Anyhow, it's over, and everyone learned a lesson."

"A lesson?"

Larry smiled faintly. "Maybe two, sir. The farmers learned a Texas trail-herd's not to be monkeyed with. The Texans learned that not all range land is open—at least around Olanthe."

"And you—what did you learn?"

"I have to do a lot more than just *sell* railroad land."

Reeves reached into a humidor on the small, bolted-down stand beside his chair, took a cigar, and offered one to Larry. "I hope you have at least one vice, Mr. Crane."

"Several of them, sir, including a fine cigar."

Larry accepted the warm, brown tube, carefully cut off the end, rolled it about in his lips. Then he struck a match, and Reeves leaned toward the flame. Larry eased back and luxuriously pulled on the fine Havana. Reeves watched him through a cloud of soft, blue smoke. He broke the silence. "What more must you do, Mr. Crane?"

Larry considered, looking out the window. "I

have to change people's lives—at least here in Olanthe. They don't like farmers."

"Considering the full stock pens out there, I don't blame them."

"Nor do I. But it has to change. The Chicago and Far Western is forcing it on them."

"Oh? How so?"

Larry eyed Reeves with disbelief. Then he gestured around the palatial room in which they sat. "This symbolizes it. You've brought Chicago, and set it down right here. Sooner or later, we'll bring San Francisco and Santa Fe and Los Angeles to Olanthe, Kansas. There will be a railroad through the Texas cattle country, and then the herds won't come here. What then?"

"You answer, Mr. Crane. You asked the question."

"Olanthe doesn't know it, but it's changing right now. This soil is for raising wheat, sir." Larry's face fired with eagerness. Reeves calmly watched him. "Rich farms, sir! Olanthe, the market center!" His face fell. "But they don't see it."

"Or won't?"

"No, none of them is stupid, at least the merchants and saloonkeepers. They came out with end-of-track when the railroad was building, so they have guts and brains. They took a chance, and they won. Now, it's just that they can't see the signs of change yet. So they don't like what I see in store for them."

Reeves moved his cigar in his fingers. "Any reason they should? You've started to cut up open range. You've drawn a gun on a Texas trail crew, and watched their cattle stampede. You—"

"Pardon, sir. The Texans held guns on the farmers, and were about to kill them—at least, one of the crew was. So I threw a gun on him to stop trouble. Then, after Flying W was headed safely for the pens again, I read the riot act to the farmers. They didn't like me, either—after that."

Reeves grunted. "So they *both* hate the railroad."

Larry considered the great man with a steady probing that Reeves met with challenging eyes. Larry, leaning forward, slowly rubbed his hands together.

"Chicago and Far Western gets no traffic between here and the Coast. What it gets here comes once a year—cattle. The railroad has to have traffic all the year around—grain and produce, farming equipment, and shipments to merchants, and passengers. So far as Olanthe is concerned, it's up to me to bring that about."

"By antagonizing everyone, Mr. Crane?"

Larry answered levelly, "You don't believe that, Mr. Reeves. The farmers would stop cattle coming to Olanthe, so the herds would go to some other railroad. We can't lose that business—yet. The Flying W would have killed the farmers, and so no more would come to buy railroad land.

Either way, we lose. I move and speak softly, sir. I try to get respect for the railroad. But this was one time a gun and strong words were needed. I did what I had to do."

Reeves sent a blue cloud into the air. For a long moment, Larry expected the quiet little man to explode.

Reeves slowly withdrew the cigar from his lips. "Gerald Marlowe hired you, didn't he?"

Larry could not quite hide his surprise. "In Kansas City."

"How old are you?"

"Thirty, next May."

"College?"

"Yes, sir. Virginia Military."

"Southerner! Fought in the War?"

"From right after First Bull Run to Appomattox. Fortieth Virginia Cavalry."

"Commission?"

"Yes, sir, but just a plain trooper at first. Captain, at the end."

"And then you came west?"

"Yanks didn't leave much of my town, sir, including my father's tobacco warehouse. Mother and Father died during the War."

"Did Marlowe tell you what he had in mind?"

"Just that I was to be land agent here in Olanthe, maybe some place else later on—a better spot for land sales, if I work out here."

Reeves pulled on his cigar a moment. "You're

right, Mr. Crane. I wondered if you'd agree with me just because I happen to be what I am. You didn't. Nor did you blame anyone. Yes, I imagine you do walk and talk softly, as you put it. But you acted fast—and correctly—when you had to. You'll do."

"Thank you, sir."

Reeves arose. The little man looked thoughtfully out the window. "You see the future here the way I do, Mr. Crane. What about the country west?"

"Basically, the same, sir. Not all farms, of course, but mines and lumbering, about anything you can think of. Towns and cities, too. The railroad will bring 'em if we get the chance."

Reeves nodded slowly. "Yes, you'll do, Mr. Crane. Marlowe told me about you, and now I have plans myself. Handle this and—but let's see."

He extended his hand. "Thanks for coming, Mr. Crane. I'll watch your work through your reports to Marlowe. But before I leave here, we'll go over your work to date."

Again, Larry felt the amazing strength of the fleshy hand. Reeves called Blogget, who appeared as though shot from a cannon. "Blogget, I believe Mr. Crane might enjoy a box of cigars. See that he gets one."

"Yes, Mr. Reeves."

Larry followed Blogget into the corridor, and to the end of the car.

The door of one of the compartments suddenly

opened. A woman stood within, her slender hand on the knob. Larry glimpsed deep-brown eyes, round with surprise, and rich full lips. Her tall, full, curved body was wrapped in a night robe, which was tied at the neck. She was young, about twenty. Dark hair cascaded about her shoulders and down her back. Her face was oval, cheekbones high, nose small but well-formed. Then he saw the eyes again—dark, deep, and knowing. They lighted with an inner fire, and then she stepped back, and the door closed with a thud.

Larry looked questioningly at Blogget, who motioned him forward, and spoke in a low tone, over his shoulder. "That's Miss Harriet, sir—Mr. Reeves' niece."

Larry threw a look back at the closed door. "He has everything, doesn't he?"

"Oh, yes, sir!"

Larry swung off the last step of the car and, stepping across the rails of the main line, strode away toward the town. Behind him, a green drape was pulled aside. A portion of a lovely face appeared, and brown eyes followed his progress.

Harriet Reeves released the drape, and slowly turned back into the stateroom. Her cheeks pulled in, and her dark, smooth brow arched as she moved with slow step, eyes alight. She turned to her maid, who was making the bed. "Who was that?"

The maid looked blank. Harriet added impatiently, "The man who was just with Uncle?"

"I don't know, Miss."

Harriet smiled, and her lips moved thoughtfully. "Tall . . . not bad looking . . . and strong. I don't know who he is, either. But . . . Marie . . . I'm going to know."

# IX

As Larry left the special car, crossed the tracks, and started back to his office, another pair of eyes watched him. Pardee Malan had awakened early, with a splitting headache and temper to match. He had lost money last night at a poker table, had too many drinks and his last memories were torturous ones of finding his way to his room. He had awakened to look on bare pine boards that served as walls, and he could hear the man's snores next door as plainly as if the unknown slept in the bed beside him.

Pardee tried to sleep, couldn't, cursed the hotel, and the ill luck that had brought him here. He swung out of bed, stepped to the window, blinking against the harsh light. When his eyes focused, he saw the slender figure walking, with long easy stride, across the wide, barren space that separated the railroad from the town proper. Pardee's face tightened, and a harsh glint flicked in his eyes as he recalled the man's gun held on him and, later, the fight in the hotel hallway.

Pardee's lips curled angrily back from his teeth. There should be some way that score could be evened. Here, Pardee stood in a flea-bag hotel when he should be at the best one in town. Of course, that was Denbo's fault, and now Pardee's hatred had a second target. He should even the score with both of them. As he watched Crane disappear, his forehead was creased, eyes distant and steely. A dozen ideas for revenge flicked into his mind only to be flicked out again. He cursed, turned, dropped on the bed. Now, if he had been trail boss, and Denbo . . .

Pardee's head lifted with the shock of the new thought. Why not be trail boss? Why not go back to Texas as Flying W foreman, and leave Denbo here, without a job and discredited? Pardee almost forgot his headache as he sat, a ludicrous figure in long underwear, on the edge of the hard bed, and tried to bring out the vague idea that had popped into his head. He couldn't do it alone. But he had friends in all these crews that now gathered in Olanthe. How? Pardee settled down to hard thinking.

Larry spent the morning writing answers to more land queries, set a date for a man coming from Illinois, and another from Michigan. He felt hopeful about the morning's work as he arose, pulled on his coat, and left for the hotel and the noon meal.

Reeves' suggestions echoed in his mind as he entered the crowded dining room, and found a seat at one of the tables. Kathy passed him several times, from kitchen to table, and back again. He smiled and she answered, but did not have time to speak. Maybe tonight, after dinner, he could outlast the loafers on the porch, and have a few moments with her. Supported by that hope, he finished his meal, and arose. As he headed for the lobby, Denbo moved down the aisle from another table, and joined him. Together, they walked into the lobby.

Denbo said, "Have you seen that gewgawed car on the siding? Must've cost all of Texas, the way it's painted up."

"I've seen it. I was there this morning. And it didn't cost quite that much—maybe half of Texas."

"Sure is something!" Denbo looked sharply at Larry. "You were there? In it? What kind of man rides around in a thing like that!"

"A railroad vice-president. He's boss of my boss."

"Now ain't you something—knowing people like that!"

"I don't know him—like a friend, if that's what you mean. It was strictly business, and it will be the next time I go."

"Next time!" Denbo whistled softly, in envy. He wanted to know what the car was like inside, and Larry told him. Denbo said, "This is one time I wish I was you and I've never said that before. Be something, just to pass: the morning with folks who can live like that."

"Mr. Crane?"

Larry and Denbo turned to face Blogget. He carried a bowler hat respectfully in his hand, and his myopic, washed-blue eyes fawned behind the pince-nez. "You weren't in your office. I'm glad I found you."

"Does Mr. Reeves want me?" Larry asked.

"No—well, in a way, yes, Mr. Crane. It's really Miss Reeves."

"Miss Reeves!"

"She wonders if you would be so good as to show her around the town. Mr. Reeves agreed that you'd be a proper guide." Larry stared, and Blogget hurried on. "Could you attend on Miss Reeves at the car—say, at two o'clock?"

Larry's voice caught. "Of course."

"Thank you, sir. Miss Reeves will be pleased when I tell her."

He bowed, turned, and hurried out of the hotel, Larry and Denbo staring after him. Denbo broke the stunned silence first. "Attend on a lady! Show her around town! And she lives in that car?"

Just then, Kathy passed the doorway. Larry made a grimace. Denbo said, amazed, "You sure don't look pleased. Now me . . . !"

"I wish I could be," Larry said, then turned on his heel and headed for his room.

Just before the appointed hour, Larry left the hotel, shirt changed, shoes shined, and suit brushed. He felt relieved that Kathy was not in sight as he crossed the lobby and porch, and strode off toward the railroad station.

Blogget opened the varnished door at Larry's knock, murmured a polite word of greeting, and took him along the corridor to a door. He knocked, and the door opened.

Harriet Reeves stood framed, her long, graceful arm still extended to the door knob. She wore a light gray dress, the skirt rustling in long, soft folds from her narrow waist to the toes of her shoes. Her dark hair was piled high atop her head, dark ringlets hanging before each small ear. Larry was instantly aware of red lips and an olive skin, of high cheekbones delicately rounded. Her dark and knowing eyes held on him, seemed to pierce deep. Blogget made the introductions, and she spoke in a low, musical voice.

"I'm so glad you could come, Mr. Crane. I'm afraid I've imposed on your time."

"Not at all!"

She stepped aside. "But do come in, Mr. Crane. Perhaps we could have tea before we start our exploration?"

Larry found himself seated on a costly chair in a miniature drawing room. A maid in a demure black dress, trimmed with white, brought the tea things and Harriet Reeves, seated in a chair across the small table, poured and served, after dismissing the maid.

The almost-forgotten courtesies of Virginia

came back to Larry with a rush. The girl put him at ease, and yet her charm kept disturbing him. He was aware that she endeavored to charm men out of their wits. Jepson Reeves' niece could be as dangerous as a stick of dynamite with a sputtering fuse. She must have pumped her uncle, for she seemed familiar with Larry's work and his background. She asked about Kansas, Olanthe, Larry's life.

"It must be very exciting," she exclaimed. "It's so—so—primitive out here! So adventurous! All those cowboys! Are there any Indians?"

Not in Olanthe, he told her, but they could be found within a day's ride from town. He sketched his work, told her the town's history. She listened with fascination, and her eyes, dancing with excitement, bothered him. He was glad when, at last, she clapped her slender hands, and exclaimed, "But let's go see it all—now!"

He waited for her on the station platform. She soon joined him, a pert bonnet, with a small plume, atop her pile of hair. He helped her down the steps, and she opened a bright parasol, placed her arm in his, and smiled. "Now! Our adventure."

First, she wanted to know about the row of buildings fronting the tracks.

"They're rough, and I wouldn't dream of even taking you near them," Larry answered. "The cowboys celebrate there."

She studied them as though she would like to dare propriety, and examine them, anyhow. As they walked slowly along, Larry was conscious of curious eyes from store and house windows. Ace Clemson came yawning out of his office, stopped dead, and his mouth snapped shut as he stared at them.

Larry showed her his office. She stood close as he pointed to the map, explaining the red rectangles marking his first sales. A subtle perfume wrapped about him. He was glad to escape to the street, but started when she indicated the hotel.

He was relieved that Kathy and her mother were out of sight, but one man sat in the shade of the verandah. At their approach the man arose, stood watching, and then came down the steps into the sunlight.

Brace Denbo grinned at Larry. "Howdee," he said.

Harriet's fingers tightened on Larry's arm. She leaned toward him, and whispered, "A cowboy! Do you know him? I'd like to talk to a real live cowboy."

Larry took off his hat, and made the introduction. "Miss Reeves, may I present Mr. Denbo? He is in charge of the Flying W herd from Texas."

Denbo's handsome face lighted as he swept off his hat and made a bow. Denbo looked admiringly at the girl, who said, "It is a pleasure, Mr. Denbo. I never thought I'd meet someone from Texas, and a cowboy!"

"Well, ma'am, you'll find lots of Texas cowboys around Olanthe right now."

"But I'm sure not many in charge of a whole herd!"

"I ain't—I'm not. It's sold, and I'll be heading back to Texas, soon."

Harriet made a pout. "Your herd's gone. I would have liked to see one, out on the range, as Mr. Crane calls it."

Denbo brightened. "Now, ma'am, maybe you could. That is, if you don't mind riding out with me, south of town."

The girl frowned prettily. "I don't know, Mr. Denbo. Perhaps my uncle would object and—" Denbo waited breathless, then she smiled. "But I'll ask him. Can I get word to you?"

"Easy, ma'am. Here to the hotel, or send a man looking around the Texas Saloon, down near the pens." He bowed again. "I'll sure expect word— maybe, tomorrow?"

"You'll not think me bold, Mr. Denbo?"

"No, ma'am!"

Harriet smiled, and moved on, Larry beside her. It took but a few moments to walk to the far end of the street. The roadway ended at the edge of a sea of grass extending to the horizon, and Larry told her there was nothing north but plains, scattered Indians, and diminishing buffalo.

Larry assisted her up the steps of the car. She turned on the platform, and put out her hand. "You have been so kind, Mr. Crane."

Her gaze moved along the façade of the town across the tracks. "Do you think I'll be quite safe with Mr. Denbo?"

"Why, I should think so. Out here, he holds a responsible position."

"I'm so glad, then. I'll ask Uncle. Just imagine what my friends will say, back home, when I tell them I was with a cowboy!"

Her face glowed with anticipation. Larry said dryly, "He's more than a curiosity."

Her eyes lifted, contrite. "But, Mr. Crane, I know that. He's a very handsome man, isn't he?"

That evening, Denbo did not appear in the dining room, and, to Larry's relief, Kathy did not seem to have heard about Harriet Reeves. Larry walked out on the porch after the meal.

Twilight was approaching, and he heard a locomotive whistle, a clank of couplings, and knew another shipment was starting east. He left the hotel, and strolled down toward the honkytonk area. A word of warning about Harriet Reeves' character might help Denbo to see his situation clearly.

Night fell swiftly. Larry heard the night's celebrations beginning. As he turned the corner, he saw a band of riders come round the far end of the pens, and spur their horses toward the saloons. A gun spat a tongue of red flame as a cowboy fired into the air. Dust swirled over Larry with a drum-rolling of hoofs, and then the band streaked on to a sliding halt before a long hitchrack.

Ace Clemson appeared beside Larry, and studied the street ahead, weighing it for trouble as he chewed on a toothpick. He said, at last, "Might be a quiet night. With luck."

"I'd say, you'd need all the luck you can get."

"Always do. But it sort of feels right, tonight. Lot of noise, a few drunks, that'll be all."

"Seen Brace Denbo?"

"Early afternoon. About the time you and that fine lady were walking around." He indicated the private car, hidden now by darkness, off across the barren area. "She come from there, didn't she?"

"That's right. But you haven't seen Denbo lately?"

"Nope." The marshal continued to study the street. "I keep the peace, such as it is, in Olanthe."

Larry looked around in surprise. "What do you mean?"

"You—and the important gent over in that car—you both have started some bad feelings."

"That again!"

Now Ace turned and faced him squarely. "More'n that, Crane. You're looking for Denbo. I'm trying to tell you, if you—or him—start trouble, I'll jail you, him, or both of you so fast you'll be dizzy."

"Now what in the world makes you think—?"

"There won't be trouble? Crane, I've heard the talk, just like you have. Them farmers! When Flying W starts talking about taking care of them, of you and your office, that means a lot more'n a drunk getting quarrelsome. There ain't going to be a war in Olanthe. Get that straight!"

He strode off, leaving Larry standing in stunned amazement.

# X

Larry strode after Ace, anger mounting with every step. He caught up with the marshal, a few yards from the lighted entrance of the Texas Saloon. Noise of laughter, voices, and a beating piano forced Larry to raise his voice as the marshal turned to face him.

"Who told you that?"

Ace peered at him. "It's the first you've heard it?"

"That's right—and I want to know who's making threats."

Ace lifted his hat, and scratched his forehead. "I reckon Flying W. I heard it at Overman's, and again at Tatum's. Seems like it's all over town."

"You said Denbo—"

"I just figured it. He speaks for Flying W, don't he?"

"Let's find out—and start at the Texas."

Larry whipped about, and strode to the saloon, flailed back the batwings, and stepped inside. Ace followed him, and came through the doorway as Larry halted a few steps inside. The place was crowded, most of the tables taken, and men lined the bar. Larry searched for Denbo, moved slowly toward the bar, looking toward the far tables, searching the shifting crowd.

Noise beat at his ears, and tobacco smoke

tangled in low, sluggish blue streamers. One of the hostesses stopped and smiled, but Larry waved her on. He went to the bar, and still no glimpse of Denbo. Cowboys milled about the bar in a gay mood, and readily made way for Larry. He finally reached the bar, and Bat Owens asked, "What's yours?"

"A shot—and is Brace Denbo around?"

"Ain't seen him." Bat Owens turned away, and then placed the filled glass before Larry. "But there's some Flying W over there."

He indicated a corner of the huge room, beyond the crowd. Larry paid for the drink, downed it, and turned to push back through the crowd. A shifting of the crowd revealed a table near the wall, and Larry glimpsed Pardee Malan, then the crowd blocked the scene again.

He worked his way down the aisle. Ace Clemson followed him a few steps back, allowing men to come between them, then moving on, finally easing back as Larry came to a halt before the table.

Pardee Malan glanced up, and saw him. He met Larry's eyes with a challenging stare, and then deliberately looked away, ignoring him. Larry did not recognize the other four men at the table as Flying W crewmen, but that meant nothing.

He said, "Malan."

Malan looked up, then dropped back in his chair, and waited deliberately. Larry moved toward him around the table, aware of the others'

111

resentment. He looked down at Pardee. "I'd like to talk to you—private."

"There's nothing we got to say."

Larry snapped, "But you've things to say—behind my back."

Malan's eyes blazed a second, then hooded, and he shrugged. "You're not talking sense."

"Let's find out. Is it true Flying W is making threats against me and those farmers you ran up against?"

"I've heard something like that," Malan answered evenly.

"Then you are threatening?"

"Me? Not me, but that don't say I wouldn't like to see those sodbusters run out. It just might happen, too."

"That might take some doing."

Malan grinned, and slowly stood up, pushed his chair back. "I said before, I'd like an even chance at you. Is that what you're wanting? Sure be glad to accommodate."

The marshal pushed between them, speaking quietly. "Sit down, Malan. Crane, back off."

Malan stood studying the marshal, and looking longingly at Larry. His hand rubbed along his trouser leg, eager to grasp the holstered gun a scant inch from his fingers. Then he spat to one side into the sawdust floor, and sat down. "Another time, I reckon."

The marshal turned to Larry. "I said, back off."

"You know why I'm here, Ace. I want to know if he started those threats. If he didn't, who did?"

Malan, leaning to one side to clear Clemson, said, "Why don't you ask Brace? He ramrods this bunch."

The marshal stood adamant, and Malan straightened, then eased back in his chair. Larry balanced a moment, and then turned on his heel, and walked away down the aisle. Behind him, the marshal remained stationary until Larry had disappeared in the crowd. Then he turned, and looked down at Malan.

"I told him. Now I'm telling you, and you pass it on to your boys and Denbo. I don't hold with him bringing in farmers to rangeland. But I don't hold to gun fights and raids, either. If any of you figure on a fight, just figure me in on it, too. Anyone starts a-shooting will end up facing me. That goes for both sides."

Malan nodded, shrugged. "Like I told the dude, find Denbo, and do your talking."

"And that, I will."

Larry went out the door into the night. Men milled along the beaten dirt sidewalk, their faces lit up by the lamplight streaming from every building. Watching for Denbo, Larry moved along with the human current, entered the next place, a gambling hall. Denbo was not there, nor could Larry find him at any of the dives and dens along the street.

He returned to the hotel, went to Denbo's room, and knocked on the door. After repeated knocking, with no answer, Larry started to his own room, and then changed his mind. He would wait for Denbo down on the porch.

The porch was filled with men enjoying the soft evening breeze, but Larry found a chair at one end, and sat down. Light streamed out the open door from the lobby. He could see anyone coming in, so he set himself to patient waiting.

Time passed. One by one, the men left for their rooms, and at last, Larry sat alone. He moved to a chair near the steps. The stores along the street grew dark, and at last he felt as if he had the town to himself, except whenever a shout came from the honkytonks.

A shadow suddenly crossed the lamplit doorway, and Larry jumped to his feet. Kathy came out. She stopped in surprise, and then came over to take the chair Larry held for her.

She said, "It seems forever, since I've had a chance to sit on the porch."

"You need more help in the kitchen and the rooms."

"From where? No servant girls come out to this country to look for work. Even if they did, what would I do with one after this rush is over?"

He nodded, but made no further comment, though it was on the tip of his tongue. Instead he asked, "Have you seen Denbo since supper?"

"Not since noon. He said he would be out on the range until tomorrow sometime."

Larry made a small, disappointed sound. "I'll see him then, I guess."

Silence fell between them until Kathy said hesitantly, "I hear the girl who lives in the fine railroad car is very pretty."

Larry started, answered quickly, "Yes. Of course, she's Chicago society, and not our kind. All of us are something like curios to her."

"I heard you showed her about the town. I would have liked to have seen her."

"Yes, I . . . well, her uncle requested it and he's my boss."

"But I imagine it wasn't very difficult."

Larry moved uncomfortably. "A job and— no, not as hard as some I've had. But I'm glad it's over." He hesitated, then said quickly, "Mr. Reeves is interested in what I'm doing."

"I'm glad. But then, he should be, shouldn't he?"

"I mean, more interested than I expected. I think he might have something in mind for me and the town. Something much better."

"I hope so." She sighed wearily, and stood up. Larry jumped to his feet. "What has he in mind for Mr. Denbo?"

"What?"

"I hear Mr. Denbo is quite smitten with the young lady, too. So, naturally, I wonder if his

115

interest is not so much in her—as you inferred, for yourself."

He stared, not knowing quite what to say, and she turned to the door. "From what I heard, the young lady has values quite her own. Good night, Mr. Crane."

She was gone, and Larry strode to the door, caught himself up, and made a sound under his breath. He dropped into the chair, and frowned on the dark street.

Denbo did not appear in the dining room the next morning, and Kathy, busy as usual, gave him a smile as though they had spoken of the weather last night. Larry left for his mail at the station, and then returned to his office, watching for Denbo. Incredible as it seemed in a town so small, he had no glimpse or word of Denbo until late afternoon.

Larry had gone to Reeves' railroad car, answering a request through Blogget, and had spent an hour going over the work he had done so far. Reeves listened, asked shrewd questions. He thanked Larry, at the end of the report, and that was that. Larry felt let-down.

At the station, Ross signaled through the window that there were no wires from Chicago, and Larry started across the barren area to the street.

Just then, two horses rounded the far end of the pens. Larry stopped short when he saw one was a woman, riding side-saddle, a rarity in this country. A split-second later, he recognized Harriet Reeves and Brace Denbo. Harriet saw Larry, and called him over.

Harriet's cheeks were red from riding into the wind, and her eyes danced. Denbo nodded coldly to Larry, and then looked at Harriet, with positive infatuation.

Harriet said excitedly, "Mr. Crane! I've been out on the range! I've eaten with cowboys at a—a—chuckwagon, isn't that it, Bra—Mr. Denbo?"

"That's it," Brace grinned widely.

"They'll never believe me in Chicago unless"—she turned her deep eyes on Denbo—"unless I take Mr. Denbo along to prove it."

Denbo's smile grew still wider. She began to dismount, and Larry helped her down. Denbo looked unhappy at this. Larry stepped back, and bowed. "It must have been wonderful, Miss Reeves. Glad you had the chance to see how we live out here." He turned to Denbo. "See you at the station in a few minutes?"

"Sure."

Larry bowed again to Harriet, and strode off.

From the station platform, Larry watched Harriet and Denbo's farewell. Harriet climbed the steps, posed prettily at the top, and disappeared into the coach. Denbo stood, hat in hand, and then reluctantly gathered up the reins, and led the two horses to the station. Larry stepped out to meet him.

Denbo flashed an irritated look at Larry. Then

117

he drew a deep breath, and thumbed his hat up on his forehead. "Now, there's as fine a woman as I ever met, bar none."

"Little rich for our kind, isn't she?"

"You'd think it, sure enough. But she ain't. Just as natural and sweet."

"I'm glad to hear it. But she's still rich, and from Chicago."

"Now what does that mean?"

"Just a passing thought. Something more important on my mind—about you and Flying W."

Denbo, still walking beside Larry and leading the horses, turned his head. "What about?"

Larry halted, and Denbo turned to face him. Perplexedly, Larry studied the rugged, open face. "Talk and whispers, Denbo. They're around. Let them go, and they get bigger and bigger. I've been told that Flying W—or you—intend to do something about me and the farmers out there. Those are almost the exact words as I heard them. I decided to come direct to you. Truth? or lies?"

Denbo's eyes narrowed. He laughed dryly. "True—but I reckon, not the way you heard it. Flying W does figure on doing something."

"Such as?"

"Remember, I asked you who could buy your damn farmland? Well, I sent a telegram to my boss. I told him what I thought we ought to do. He's on his way up here—or will be, soon."

"For what?"

Denbo laughed loudly, and dropped his hand on Larry's shoulder. "Man, you act like we was coming after you with all guns blazing, or with hangropes flying." He sobered. "Four, five years ago, my boss and me made a drive up here. We both liked the look of the range. Grass thick, and good for beef. We talked about setting up a northern ranch, registering our Flying W brand right here in Kansas. Did nothing, and then I find what you and the railroad figure to do. So I wired the boss. I got an answer two days ago but—" he looked back to the railroad car—"but my mind got on something else and, besides, there was plenty of time."

"Time to do what?" Larry demanded impatiently.

"Why, find out how much an acre you want for this railroad land, and buy it up—all of it. Make the first steps, anyhow, until the boss can get up here and put his brand on it."

"You! Flying W! buying—"

"Why not? If it's good enough for farming, it sure as hell is good for beef. That's what we always thought." Denbo tightened the reins in his hands. "Right now, I aim to get these horses back to Tatum, and then have a drink before dinner. You figure what it'll cost, and I'll see you, come morning, in your office."

He lengthened his stride, leaving Larry statue-still with surprise.

# XI

Larry went directly to his office, closed the door, and turned to the big map. Two small rectangles of red marked Briggs and Whelan—and Flying W wanted all the rest! One purchase—all of it!

What was he to do? He dropped into the chair before his desk and kept staring at the map. Distractedly he rubbed his hand along his jaw and across his face. He must not, at any cost, go to Reeves. Larry Crane, and no one else, must make this decision.

For a whole hour, Larry paced the office, stood at the window staring out on the dirt street, and returned to his desk. Finally, he swept up his hat, and left the office for the hotel. As he stepped up on the porch, Denbo came out. The trail boss looked brushed, polished, and eager, and he lighted up when he saw Larry.

"*Amigo*! You can't guess what's happened to this cowpoke! I been invited to that fancy car for a fancy meal—Miss Reeves and her uncle."

"Congratulations," Larry answered sourly.

Denbo laughed, and gave him a prod in the belly with his thumb. "No call to get down in the mouth, friend. You had your turn, and now I got mine."

Denbo went lightly down the steps, and strode away, toward the railroad car. Larry went to his room, and thoughtfully removed his coat and tie, rolled up his sleeves, and washed his hands and face in the big china bowl, with water poured from the handsome, ungainly pitcher.

He brushed his hair, replaced his tie, and went down to supper. He ate without really tasting his food, then wandered out onto the porch, stood at the top of the steps for a long moment, then walked directly to where the street ended abruptly in grass.

As twilight deepened, he stood there, looking northward over the green land. Darkness settled, the stars came out, and Larry stood there motionless, trying to see the future. Finally, he took a deep breath, and exhaled with a long, triumphal sigh. His decision was made.

Next morning, Denbo came into Larry's office. Larry rose, and pointed to the chair beside his desk. Denbo dropped into it.

"How was your evening?" Larry asked.

"Never had anything like it. No place in Texas puts that kind of food on the table. Do they live that way every day?"

"Even better. That's just a railroad car."

"Makes a man wonder, don't it!" Denbo's face cleared. "But mighty fine folks, those Reeves. Knew how Harriet was, but her uncle surprised me. No bigger'n a bull-calf, but you can tell he's king of his range, sure enough. I like him, though, and I think he likes me."

"That helps."

Denbo nodded, and his expression changed. "Now, I guess, we're to talk business. I want a price on that range, south of here. Understand it's reasonable, and if that's so, I can put the brand on it now."

Larry went to the map, and indicated the block of railroad land. "You want all of this?"

"That's right."

Larry touched the two red rectangles. "Briggs and Whelan own these parcels, right in the middle of what you want to buy. That's a problem for you."

"Not much. We can buy 'em out."

"What if they don't want to sell?"

"They will, once Flying W's all around 'em."

Larry went to his chair and sat down, then leaned across the desk, and folded his hands on the top. Then he said calmly, "We're not selling to Flying W—or any other ranch."

Denbo's mouth fell open, then snapped shut. "Why not? We got the money. No argument, if the price is reasonable. You said anybody could buy."

"I did—if the buyer is the kind we want."

Denbo's face grew purplish-tan. "You're saying we ain't the kind of outfit you'd want around here? Flying W's the biggest spread in our part of Texas and—"

"Brace, I don't deny it." Larry went to the map, and ranged his hand over the section. "You'd buy all this and—"

"Maybe more, in a year or two. Other spreads down there are looking—"

"One outfit, Brace, one ranch—and its crew. Maybe, one more—two at the most. Cattle shipment once a year. It's not what we want."

"You want to sell land, damn it!"

"For a reason, Brace. We want the town and the country to grow. Listen, here's the way we see it." He explained while Denbo listened frostily. But Larry went doggedly on, and concluded: "There it is. One ranch—two at the most, your way. If we keep to the original plan, we bring in many farms, many people, year-round business for the railroad and the town. Olanthe will grow and, we hope, in time will become a city."

Denbo sat silently, his eyes boring into Larry's. Then he drawled very slowly, "You're saying you're not selling to Flying W?"

"That's right. And I'm sorry."

Slowly, Denbo stood up. "You sure will be, Crane. I ain't taking your refusal. I figure Reeves is the man I want to deal with, and since last night, that won't be no problem. They like me, and they'll listen—and I'm coming, with money in my hand. You'll hear from me—or your boss."

He turned on his heel, and strode out. Larry sank back in his chair and, despite his will to

123

keep calm, almost trembled with misgivings. Gradually, he pulled himself together and then, all at once, slapped his hand down on the desk. Nothing to do but wait—so he went back to his day's work. From time to time, he glanced up and down the street anxiously, despite himself. When time for closing came, Larry felt immense relief, and rushed to the hotel.

Denbo did not show up at supper. Larry could only ponder what Denbo's absence might mean. It might well be that, right at this moment, Denbo was supping with Reeves in the railroad car and, over a fine cigar, clinching the land deal for Flying W. The thought turned Kathy's fluffed potatoes to alum in his mouth.

Next morning, he had no more than stepped into his office, when Blogget appeared, to say he was wanted at the car. Hiding his nervousness as best he could, Larry went with Blogget, and once more was ushered into the palace on wheels. Reeves waved him to a chair with a gesture that Larry knew could mean only one thing—suppressed anger.

"Mr. Crane, I'll come directly to the point. I understand you have been given an offer for all our remaining land here."

"Yes, sir—yesterday. Mr. Denbo, for the Texas ranch, Flying W. They want to establish a northern range."

"And . . . ?"

"I turned it down."

"So I've heard. I've wondered why—since I'm right here in town—you didn't speak to me, or ask my advice about it."

Larry came near to wilting altogether beneath the withering glance of the little emperor with the round face. "I didn't come, sir, because I felt that all the standards for land development out here had been set up—Marlowe told me, there have been letters from Chicago, and you and I seemed to be in agreement when we last talked here. This sale conflicted with everything in our policy."

"Still, Mr. Crane, it's quite large and, as I said, I'm right here in town."

"That's right, sir. But I felt the decision was up to me, without running here for advice. Suppose you had not been in town, sir? I would have had to make my decision anyway. I didn't turn Mr. Denbo down without a lot of thought."

So slowly that Larry, at first, was not aware of it, Reeves' features softened, and his small lips moved into a smile. "Very good, Mr. Crane. The sale would have defeated our whole purpose, and you acted on your own, and correctly. Mr. Denbo was most unhappy, but I confirmed your decision."

Larry couldn't hold back his ever-so-slight whistle, and Reeves' smile broadened. Then he sobered. "Mr. Denbo was more than unhappy.

He threatened us. I think something just before our talk had upset him very badly. Point is, you may be having trouble here over this—from Mr. Denbo. Can you handle it?"

"I think so, sir."

"I'll keep in close touch, though I'm leaving, this afternoon, to look over our land and prospects further west."

"I'm sorry you're going, sir."

"Thank you, Mr. Crane. I hope to see you again. I'll be watching your reports with a good deal of interest. It has been a pleasure to meet you."

He rose and extended his hand, which Larry took with more fervor than he intended to show. He moved toward the door, but Reeves checked him. "Oh, I believe my niece wants to thank you for your courtesy. Blogget will show you. Goodbye, sir, and good sales—many of them."

At Blogget's knock, Harriet opened the door of a small drawing room. She dismissed Blogget, and closed the door after him. Indomitable flirt that she was, Larry couldn't help but see that she was very much upset, even while bestowing on him her thanks for guiding her around the town.

Larry smiled at her thanks, which seemed to have no end. "I'll be sorry to see you go, Miss Reeves. I'm sure Mr. Denbo will, too."

Suddenly she looked confused and more than half angry, then she shrugged. "I doubt if he will. Are all Texas men presumptuous, Mr. Crane?"

"Presumptuous?"

She blushed. "It would seem so. I had thought Mr. Denbo would be a kind and perfect escort. And, of course, I wanted to see everything I could, so I went with him to the holding grounds. But, apparently, Mr. Denbo thought this gave him certain rights. He had ideas, with no basis in fact. Nothing I said or did should have made him think—"

She broke off, half-turned to the window, and then quickly faced Larry again. "I must confess, to my horror, Mr. Denbo practically proposed. Of course, I couldn't consider it. I was very gentle, but firm. I'm sure, coming from Virginia, you understand, Mr. Crane."

"I understand," he replied flatly, then asked, "Was this before he saw your uncle?"

"Why . . . yes. He came yesterday, about noon, without invitation. I received him and . . . this came up. He left very angry, and I am sorry, believe me. But he did see Uncle."

Larry bowed his way out, and walked slowly back to the town. Now he knew why Denbo was angry!

Back at his office, he stood and studied the big wall map, with all the fervor of an empire builder. Then he grinned, and burst into laughter—at himself. "Come off it, Crane! You're a hired hand, and nothing more. It would do you good to know what Denbo and half the people in town think of you. Now get to work, and earn your pay."

He did not see Denbo for the noon meal, and that was no surprise. Denbo didn't show up for supper, either. As Larry was leaving, Kathy beckoned him toward the lobby. Surprised that she could filch even a moment from her steaming trays, Larry followed her.

She looked into the dining room to make sure no one was in earshot, and then faced Larry worriedly. "Have you seen Mr. Denbo?"

"Why, no—not since yesterday."

"I thought you might have. Three separate people have told me he's . . . I hate to say it but . . . well, he's trying to drink up the town. And—he's getting quarrelsome."

Larry pretended surprise, and played the sage counselor. "It will be all right, Kathy."

"I wish I could be sure." She became aware of his knowing look, and flushed. "Of course, he's just a guest—like you. But I'd be worried about anyone." Kathy glanced through the open door, out onto the street. "I would feel much better if I knew. I wonder, would you—?"

"I'll find out what I can."

"Thank you. I know I shouldn't ask."

"Nonsense! Perhaps, you'll be as concerned about me some day."

"Oh, I would!"

She smiled, and gave his hand a warm but

perfunctory touch, and hurried back to her chore. Larry walked out into the street, and headed for the railroad station. Doubts, doubts—was there no end to doubts?

At the street corner, he glanced toward the pens, and stopped short. The private car was gone. He heard someone behind him, and turned—it was Ace Clemson. The marshal nodded westward, along the track. "The big man left, and took his pretty filly with him."

Larry squinted at Ace Clemson's toothpick moving to the other side of his mouth. "Brace Denbo's plumb upset. She sure had him hog-tied and branded until she decided he was a cull, and threw him back on the range for someone else."

"You seem to know a lot about it," Larry grumbled.

Ace grunted, and pointed to the last saloon on the row. "Brace is down there."

"Drunk, I hear."

"That's right. Drunk—and that's all—for now. Full of talk about railroads and farmers—and you. Him and his segundo, Pardee Malan, lapping up the rotgut, and damning all sodbusters and those that bring 'em in to ruin a good range."

"Sounds like trouble."

"Talk ain't trouble, in my book. Many a man blows off pressure inside him over a bar, and no harm done. But right now, I figure the easiest way to keep it harmless is for you to stay out of Denbo's sight. You might say, that's an order. Why not head back to the hotel?"

Ace's leathery face was never firmer. Still, Larry hesitated. He didn't like the order, though he saw its reasonableness. But hadn't he gotten the information Kathy wanted? Then why not acquiesce?

"You're right, Ace. Something I *don't* want is trouble."

He turned away at Ace's slightly mocking comment. "For a man who don't want trouble, you're in the wrong job, friend. You breed it."

# XII

Larry returned to the hotel, and went directly into the kitchen to make his report. Kathy bent a solicitous ear as she toweled her hands dry before a dozen neat mountains of freshly-scoured dishes. She smiled her thanks, and set about explaining her worry.

Larry interrupted. "Don't try to explain, Kathy. If I happened to get in trouble, I'd like to know you'd want to help."

"I would, believe me."

Larry smiled, left her, and went out into the darkness of the porch. He sat there, listening to the sounds from the honkytonks. As the hotel grew silent and dark, his hope of Kathy's coming out and joining him dwindled away. He came alert when a figure came reeling around the corner, and then relaxed when Ace Clemson strode up fast through the lamplight and handled the drunken puncher.

Larry crossed the street, and questioned Ace, who answered with a shrug. "All in the night's work. That's the third sleeping it off. Their bosses will pay the fines, and that'll help toward my salary. Hope the season passes with no worse."

"What about Denbo?"

"Stopped thinking about him. I saw Malan and

some of the crew riding off south to their camp, maybe an hour ago. I figure Denbo's with 'em. He'll sleep it off. Might act a little mean for a day or two but, so long as no one crosses him, that'll be all."

"You really think so, Ace?"

"I figure the stay of the Flying W is about up. They'll be riding back to Texas, in a week or less. 'Night, Crane."

Larry watched Ace walk off, and then went to his room. He fell on the bed, and went sound asleep. His eyes snapped open to a thundering on his door.

"All right! In a minute!" he called. "Who is it?"

"Me!" a strange voice answered.

Larry threw open the door. Luke Briggs, fist upraised to strike the door again, looked at him with eyes begging in fright. Dirt streaked the boy's cheeks, and his shirt was ripped. Tears cut a jagged lacework through the dirt, and his thick chest rose and fell in gasps.

"Luke! What—?"

"Dad! The farm! Dad's shot—bad! They set fire to the house!"

Larry took the boy by the shoulder, and led him into the room. "Make sense. What's happened? Who did it?"

Luke struggled to speak coherently. "Came out! Maw's 'bout dead with worrying over Dad. The cowboys—they did it. First thing we knowed, they was riding down on us—shooting. You gotta help us!"

Larry patted the boy's shoulder, then looked high and low for his clothes, only to realize, with a jolt, that he was fully dressed. "How'd you get to town?"

"Plowhorse. Throwed a bit on it, and come in. Mr. Crane, it's awful out there!"

Larry opened a dresser drawer, took out his cartridge belt with the gun and strapped it about his waist. Then he touched the glassy-eyed boy, who was sitting hunched-up on the bed. "Luke, let's go."

Out in the hall, men stood in doorways, questioning mutely. Larry brushed by them, pulling the youth. In the rear doorway of the lobby stood Kathy, her hands sticky with dough. "What's happened, Larry?"

"I'll tell you later," he called over his shoulder, from the porch.

The plowhorse waited at the foot of the stairs. Larry ordered Luke to mount, and led the horse and boy across the street to the livery stable. He roused Tatum, saddled the bay, and headed south with Luke.

Larry had to hold his bay down to the speed of the heavier horse. Several times, he opened his mouth to question Luke, but saw it was no use, for the boy was going deeper into shock, and was barely holding on.

They encountered no riders over the vast, close-cropped plain. Here and there, an abandoned chuck wagon marked a camping site. In the distance, a wisp of smoke curled lazily upward into the morning sky. Galloping closer, Larry saw that the smoke was all that remained of the farmhouse on the hill.

Luke drummed his heels frantically into his horse's ribs. Larry let Luke ride ahead, holding his own horse to a trot. Reining left, he saw the big tent at the foot of the hill, and then the small figures of Mrs. Briggs and her daughters.

Mrs. Briggs, pale and distracted, had thrown a coat over her voluminous nightgown. Her hair fell in strings about her shoulders. Beside her stood her daughters, both ghastly pale. The tent was spotted with bullet holes, and Larry set his teeth as he swung out of the saddle, and went close to feel around one of the holes with his fingers.

Mrs. Briggs burst into tears, and came running pellmell into his arms. Larry held the woman's heavy, shaking form, and tried to calm her, and the wailing girls by her side, as he looked over her shoulder about the area.

The ground around the tent had been gouged by circling, racing hoofs. Two empty cartridge cases glinted in the torn-up dirt. Through the open tent-flap, Larry saw heavy work shoes, and empty trousers hanging near.

His hands firmed on the sobbing shoulders.

"Mrs. Briggs—Mrs. Briggs, what about your husband?"

She buried her head into his shoulder, and flung an arm toward the tent-flap. "In there—Obed's in there."

Firmly, Larry disengaged her, and she turned her back on the tent, her face in her hands. The little girls ran to her, clasping her about the legs, crying without cease. Luke was nowhere to be seen.

Larry bent, and entered. Obed Briggs lay sprawled, his clay-colored face upward, his eyes glazed. Larry knelt, and put out a finger to the dark, dried stain on the upper section of Briggs' underwear. A bullet had caught Briggs squarely in the chest, and he must have died instantly. Sunlight gleamed mockingly through the bullet holes in the tent walls, and threw golden ribbons over the raw slug-scars in the cedar treasure chest.

A sound at the rear of the tent caused Larry to look swiftly. Luke Briggs was back there, bending over a box. In his fingers gleamed something yellow and metallic, which he stuffed into his pocket. Sensing Larry's eye on him, Luke snatched up the rifle at his feet, and wheeled to go. His round, young face was distorted with haggard lines, and his eyes burned with a killing light. Larry rose. Luke tried a circling tactic, but Larry blocked him. "Where are you going?"

"Kill. Kill them. Cowboys. They murdered Dad and—"

"No, Luke. It's no good. You'll get killed, yourself."

"Let me go! Get out of my way!" Luke's maddened eyes fixed on Larry. "You started it! That day when you pulled a gun on Dad. You'd have killed him!"

Luke swung round his rifle, but was too close to line the muzzle. Larry grabbed for it, but the heavy adolescent sprang back, and brought it around again. Larry seized it, and tried to wrest it away, but madness made the boy strong beyond belief, and he forced the rifle from Larry's grip. He tried to bring the black muzzle down into aim, but Larry leapt in under, and swung. Luke's head snapped back, and his fingers opened, releasing the rifle. The boy slumped, and lay still.

Larry took up the rifle, examined Luke briefly, and left the tent. Mrs. Briggs and her daughters stood glued together, a living statue of grief. Larry took three steps toward them, when someone hailed from the distance.

Instinctively, Larry lifted the rifle, but lowered it on recognizing Whelan and his son Jory, who rode in, followed by Mrs. Whelan and her daughter. Whelan spurred his horse, and Larry strode out to meet him. "Were you attacked?" Larry demanded.

Whelan hefted the rifle he carried across the

saddle. "Drove 'em off, and think I hit one of 'em. Couldn't tell, in the half-light. Heard him yell, though."

Whelan peered toward the tent and the weeping figures. "What happened here?"

Larry told him. Mrs. Whelan, riding up, gasped with pity, and urged her horse on to the tent. She dismounted, and ran to Mrs. Briggs, while Whelan, sitting his horse, looked down and listened to Larry with the mien of an avenging prophet.

"I reckon, Luke is right, Crane. We kill us some cowboys for this."

"No, let the law handle it."

"Law? Ain't seen much of that, and what I saw was cowboy law."

Larry grasped Whelan's stirrup. "Whelan, listen! You wouldn't have a chance against those punchers. They've handled Colts and rifles all their lives. At least, let me get back to Olanthe, and see what can be done. I know the marshal will act."

"For who?"

"For you. At least, give him the chance. There's work to be done here, Whelan—Briggs has to be buried, the womenfolk taken care of. Luke will get himself killed unless an older man watches him. Let me handle the rest."

Whelan considered the tent and the weeping women, then looked back at Larry. "All right—

137

for now. But raiding and murdering can't be let go by. If there ain't some move by your lawman—"

"There will be. I promise."

"There'd better be—and damn soon. Maybe I can't stand up to one of them Texas gunslingers, but I sure can ambush, and get me a few to even the score. Better git to your lawman while I see what can be done here."

Whelan nudged his horse forward. Larry walked horse and rider to the tent. He mounted his bay, pondered over the rifle which he still held, then handed it to Whelan, who had dismounted. "This is Briggs'. But keep it away from Luke."

Whelan accepted the weapon with a bleak nod. "For a time, Crane. Luke, Jory, and me are mighty good shots."

Grim-faced, Larry neck-reined the horse, prodded a spur, and raced northward, back to Olanthe. He circled the end of the stock pens, and sped toward the marshal's office, disregarding the stares along the street. Ace Clemson met him at the door.

"Murder, Marshal," Larry snapped. "Two raids."

Ace narrowed his eyes. "Know who did it?"

"I think we both know. Anyhow, find a puncher with a bullet wound. Whelan caught him. Briggs has been killed, and both farmsteads shot up. I've kept Whelan and the boys from going on the warpath—so far. But they're not sure you're on their side."

Ace grunted. "Not as farmers, maybe. But they are citizens. We'll ride out to see the damage, and I want to see the dead man for myself. Then, I reckon, we'd better head to Flying W camp, and talk to Brace Denbo."

"He might be hard to find."

Ace started to nod, then his glance shot across the street. At the same instant, someone yelled, "Fire! Fire!"

Larry wheeled, and sprang through the doorway.

Across the way, the two windows of his small office exploded outward with a whoosh and a crash of glass, then flames and smoke came pouring out.

# XIII

Men came racing from all the buildings as smoke and flame rolled up from Larry's office. Halfway across the street, Larry realized it would be impossible to enter. Now, flames were licking toward the hotel, next door. Curious guests lined the porch railing, oblivious to the danger.

"Bucket brigade!" Larry yelled, turning to the crowd. "The hotel can catch!"

Ace Clemson raced to the general store. Overman was in the doorway, calling, "Here! Everyone! Buckets! Hurry!"

Men hurried in after Ace, and emerged, holding buckets of every kind and size. Ace directed them to the rear of the store. "There's a well and pump back there!"

Larry tried to get to his office door, but the heat drove him back, and he threw up his hand to protect his face. Smoke eddied through the broken windows, and he had an instant's view of the inferno within.

All his records were ablaze. He saw the bucket line forming from the pump behind Overman's, across the street. Looking up, he saw sparks showering on the hotel. He rushed over to the porch, with its array of gawkers.

"To the roof! Water line—quick!"

The men scattered, some vaulting over the railing to continue their gawking from a better point of view, and some falling in behind Larry as he pushed through to find Kathy and her mother standing nonplused in the lobby doorway.

Unceremoniously, Larry grabbed Mrs. Blaine, and entrusted her to one of the men who had followed him in. "Get her out on the street, away from the fire!"

He tugged at Kathy's elbow. "To the kitchen. Buckets—all kinds. Show me the pump."

"It leads from a well in the backyard." Kathy turned, and led the way.

Larry's followers thundered through the dining room into the kitchen, and grabbed up buckets. Smoke was skeining through the windows as they tramped out the rear door, behind Kathy and Larry, and raced to the well.

Larry ripped off the well cover, with two men helping. From the corner of his eye, he marked that his office was a wagging thumb of flame. The prairie wind was spilling clusters of sparks capriciously about, posing a danger, not only to the hotel, but to the entire dry, wooden structures of the town.

"Ladders—from Overman's!" he called and, with three heaves of his shoulder, catapulted three husky fellows toward the store.

Larry had one boss, whose command was crackling ever louder—that fire, next door. He seized the buckets from the men, and lined them before the well. He directed two men to work the pump handle at the same time, and added the pressure of his own shoulder. When the first ladder came, he directed its placement against the eaves at the corner of the hotel, and himself took the passed-along buckets of water, and raised them to the men mounting the ladders. He called courage to the fellows perched perilously aloft, emptying their buckets on all spots of the roof, till it was soaked through.

The office blaze crackled and roared to its peak of fury, and sent a soaring, continuing column of fire that broke, on the wind, into cherry-red swarms which came tumbling down on the hotel roof and all the ground about. The hotel's roof and walls steamed, and paint blistered out in big bubbles, but the hotel did not catch fire. Then, with an explosion of smoke, the blaze collapsed.

Flames dwindled, and died down to ineffectually licking tongues. Now, Ace Clemson's bucket men could move closer. Before long, there was only the curling upward of a few strands of blue smoke, and the dying challenge of rosy embers deep in the black rubble. Men climbed down from the high-pitched hotel roof, and threw themselves on the ground, and panted.

Larry dropped the empty pail he was holding, and swiped his arm across his sweating face. The gawkers came in to gather at the well and ask questions, and get close to the brave ones who had manned the bucket lines.

Kathy appeared at Larry's side. Her hair was hanging in tendrils over the sides of her face, and her cheeks were smudged with ash. She searched his face, with some concern. "Your office is gone. What will you do?"

"Rebuild it. Everything can be replaced."

"But your records?"

"Mostly routine. Thank God I had mailed the abstracts for Briggs and Whelan to the recorder. Lost time, but that's all."

"But how did it start?"

He shook his head slowly. "I don't know. We'll find out. You're all right, Kathy?"

"Of course! And the hotel's saved. I'll never be able to thank you."

"Thank the men of Olanthe! What about all the fellows that helped me?" He smiled wearily. "I'd better see what I can find out."

He searched out Ace Clemson through the crowd around the still-smoldering ruins of his office shack. He found Ace moving attentively from group to group of punchers and honkytonk girls.

The marshal nodded curtly toward his office, and Larry followed him out of the crowd. Ace closed the door, and grimly stationed himself in the chair before his desk. "You'd just started to tell me something. Does it fit in with the fire?"

"I think so."

Under the marshal's stern questioning, Larry told about Brace Denbo's meeting and infatuation with Harriet Reeves. He told of Flying W's offer to buy all the land, and of his own refusal, and Denbo's consequent anger. When he finished, Ace sat quite still, eyes hard and jaw set.

Finally, the marshal broke the stony silence. "Like everyone else, I'm against what you and the railroad are doing out here with that land. I can see how Denbo thought—and every puncher, for that matter. But that don't excuse what he's done—" Ace narrowed his eyes on Larry—"or what we think he's done. You admit we got no proof it's him?"

"I admit it. But I don't think it'll be hard to find."

"Maybe." Ace tapped the badge on his vest. "You know this badge ain't mine by due election. Overman, Dick Poole, and some of the others decided they needed someone to keep peace in Olanthe, since there ain't no sheriff, no county, and no means of holding an election. So, maybe, that makes it a little illegal."

"I've heard," Larry admitted.

"Still, I'm what law there is, and I always respected law. Like now—I'm for the cowboys, but I'm not for raids, burning, and murder. If I find out who did it, I'll arrest him, and I promise to turn him over to the nearest regular law officer or court. I promise that."

Larry nodded. "I accept it, Ace. Someday, Olanthe will have a court of its own, and a sheriff. I hope you'll be the lawman."

"Don't know that I'd want it, what with nothing but farmers around. Now, let's get out to the Briggs' place, and then to Flying W."

When they arrived at the destroyed farmhouse, they found Whelan and the two youths digging a grave. Whelan pulled himself out of the hole, eyed Ace suspiciously, and shook hands reluctantly. On the marshal's insistence, Whelan led the way to the tent where Briggs lay, wrapped in a blanket. Ace gently explained his duty to Mrs. Briggs, then examined the wound in Briggs' chest. Then he covered the body again. He mumbled a word of commiseration, and went outside.

Whelan said angrily, "You see it was murder. No law here." He looked at the mound of raw earth beside the gaping grave. "No doctor, no undertaker, no preacher! What kind of a town have you got, Marshal!"

Larry interposed gently, "A new town, Whelan, needing all those things. And they'll come—with your help."

"Better, first, get the killers, or there won't be nothing!"

Ace made a sign to Larry, and the two walked to their horses. They mounted, and rode off, heading westward. Ace said gloomily, after a moment, "You know—he's right, Crane. What kind of place *is* Olanthe? We've all been so busy during shipping-time, and just getting by the rest of the year, we ain't looked real hard at what we've built."

Larry glanced aside sharply, at the stony face, but said nothing.

Pursuing the marshal's plan, they rode directly to the Whelan farmstead, where they found a tent, similar to the Briggs', and the frames of a house and barn. The bullet holes in the tent told the same story. But Ace wasted no time surveying the damage. He rode out in circles about the tent, and kept bending over, watching the ground.

Finally, he reined up, and pointed to faintly-discernible tracks. "Know how to read signs?" Larry shook his head. "A round dozen, I'd say, rode up here directly from Briggs' place, back there. They circled Whelan's tent, Indian war-party style. But he was too quick and accurate with a rifle. He told you he wounded one?"

"He thinks so, at least he heard a yell."

Ace studied the ground. "They were damn careless with their signs, whoever they were. Probably figured a farmer can't trail worth shucks. They went off that way. Let's find out who they were."

Ace led off, and Larry fell in beside him. They rode north, then west. Now and then, Ace checked signs that Larry could not make out, at all. After some miles, Ace drew rein, and pointed ahead.

"Flying W camp." He turned, and looked Larry squarely in the eye. "We're riding in, but get this straight, and no argument. I do the talking—understand? Good! And keep your hand close to your Colt, but don't make a move for it until I do. Understand that?—All right, let's move in."

Ahead, a solitary chuckwagon stood in silhouette, looming larger. Then Larry saw a line of picketed horses, and a group of men sitting and standing about a cosy fire, over which hung a coffee pot. At sight of Larry and Ace, the men bunched together, with an air of sullen defiance.

Ace moved in at a steady pace, and finally drew rein, Larry beside him, at the edge of the hoof-plowed ground. Now, Larry saw blanket rolls, and all the paraphernalia of a camp. One man, lying wrapped in his blankets, lifted his pale face to watch.

"Flying W?" Ace asked, and then, quickly, "where's Denbo?"

The men shifted glances. At last, one spoke up. "Last we seen him was in town—yesterday."

"Pardee Malan?" Larry asked, catching the marshal's fleeting frown.

"He rode into Olanthe, early this morning."

Ace folded his hands over the saddlehorn, and

his sharp eyes travelled about the camp. "Where were you boys riding last night?"

Again, an exchange of shifty glances. Then the puncher answered, "From Olanthe, we came right here, and bedded down. How come the questions, Marshal?"

"Farmstead was hit south of here—two of 'em. I saw signs and a trail."

"Well, Marshal, we rode by one of them places, but it was dark and quiet. Maybe you picked our sign up by mistake. Lots of riders back and forth all the time, between here and Olanthe."

Ace pressed his lips together as his eye lingered on the man lying in his blankets. "What's wrong with him?"

"Drunk, and fell out of the saddle. Bunged up his shoulder. He'll be all right, come morning."

"Maybe I should look at him."

About the fire, the men stirred, their right hands dropping on their guns. Their spokesman said quickly, "No need, Marshal. But thank you. We take care of our own."

"But I'm curious, since bullets were flying last night, and a man was killed, over yonderly."

"Marshal, there ain't no law for you to ramrod, outside Olanthe. Like I said, Billy bunged his shoulder. We don't take kindly to your suspicion. Whyn't you and your friend pick up the right trail sign, and leave us alone?"

Ace eased back in his saddle. For a long

moment, no one moved. Finally, Ace lifted the reins. "All right, boys. But I got a memory for faces. Don't any of you show up in Olanthe, where I *am* the law. I reckon Denbo and Malan can answer questions for me."

"I reckon. Ask 'em."

Ace gave Larry a glance, and they rode off. No sound followed, and Larry checked an impulse to look back over his shoulder. Some distance out, Ace spurred his horse to an easy gallop.

"They're the ones—but no proof. And they were right, about my badge. We'll corral Denbo or Malan in town." He turned a friendly glare on Larry. "More this thing unravels, the more I find myself on your side. Why'd you ever show up in Olanthe?"

Larry smiled grimly. "No law—no nothing, as Whelan would say. Does that tell you why?"

# XIV

An hour before sunset, Larry and Ace rode back into Olanthe. By silent agreement, they headed directly for the Texas Saloon, and dismounted. They tied their horses, and pushed through the batwings.

Larry's sweeping glance along the partly-filled bar, and then among the tables, revealed neither Denbo nor Malan. He followed Ace to the bar, and Bat Owens, without a word, pushed drinks before them. "Looks like you need 'em."

Overman entered, and came over to Larry. "What caused the fire?"

"We don't know yet. Ace and I hope to find out."

Overman shook his head, and spoke gravely. "It's lucky the whole town didn't burn. All these buildings are dry as bone. I wish we could afford fire equipment or, for that matter, had enough permanent citizens to form a fire company."

"I'm hoping it'll come," Larry sighed, and downed his drink.

He perked up, upon impact of the liquor, and listened attentively as Bat informed Ace that he had seen none of the Flying W outfit since the night before. "They left—oh, maybe midnight."

"Was Denbo with them?" Larry asked.

"When they left, yes, and I never seen a feller take on so much whisky, and still be on his feet. His segundo, Malan, practically carried him out the batwings."

"So Malan was with them, too," Ace pondered.

"Trying to keep Denbo in line, I'll say that for him." Bat looked at Larry. "Don't know what you and the man in that fancy car done to him, but Brace sure breathed fire and brimstone for both of you—and them farmers, south of town."

"And visited them, too," Larry grimly informed Bat. "Both places shot up, and Obed Briggs murdered."

Bat stopped pouring a drink. He set the bottle down upon the bar without a sound, and swallowed hard, then stood, wetting his lips. Word went whispering to left and right, and the men took turns at registering stunned, stark disbelief. Ace placed his empty glass on the bar. "I'll be back, Bat. If either Denbo or Malan shows up before I do, send someone to tell me. And hold 'em here, if you have to rap a bung-stop on their skulls. They got some questions to answer."

Overman gasped. "Flying W? Mr. Denbo? Attacked and murdered?"

"We don't know, in all fairness, but we intend to find out, one way or another," Larry said, then looked at Ace. "Maybe at the other places?"

Ace led the way to Dick Poole's gambling hall, next door. Like the saloon, the place was empty, but preparations were underway for the night's wild business. Ace did not bother to stop in the main room, but continued on to a small door, and knocked. Someone called, "Come in!" Ace opened the door.

Dick Poole wheeled round from a desk where he was working over a book of accounts. He whisked it shut with a guardedness that woke suspicion. His furtive black eyes shot from Ace to Larry, and then he waved a long arm to chairs.

"Gentlemen . . . unexpected. Especially you, Crane."

Ace asked, "Have you seen Denbo and Malan?"

"Last night. Not today. Malan, at least, dropped a few chips at my tables, but Denbo's drinking didn't help my profits for the evening."

"Quarrelsome?"

Poole's lean face became unreadable. "Loud— and drunk. Said a lot of things, as I heard. I was much too busy to follow him around the place."

"Said—what?"

Poole lifted a brow to Larry. "About your friend here, and what he stands for. Frankly, I can't think of a Texan in town right now who has any love for Mr. Crane. Your farmers, sir, are unpopular."

"Very! So much so, a Texan killed one, and shot up both their farms."

Poole looked at Ace steadily, not a muscle moving in his pale face. "I take it, you feel a certain justice should be done?"

Ace exploded. "My God, Poole! What else! Can raids, arson, and murder be just let go?"

"Arson? Your office, Crane—I had hoped it was an accident and, honestly, I was a bit glad about it. But deliberately set?"

"We're sure of it."

Poole sat a moment, tapping the cover of his account book with his tapered fingers. Finally, his bloodless lips twisted, and he spoke, almost in a whisper. "The fools! The damned, idiotic fools! They've ruined themselves—and me."

Larry leaned forward, and dug at him. "What have you—"

"To do with it, Mr. Crane? My friend, can you tell me where a gambler can openly operate his business in a well-established town? Always, the law, the police, the reformers—especially the little old women in black bombazine and umbrellas, and their preachers—they all hound a clean, honest gambling hall. So I have found my niche in Olanthe."

Poole smiled at the puzzled frown on Larry's face, and at Ace Clemson's uncomprehending eyes. "Raid—arson—murder, gentlemen. And our marshal here, with no authority except the badge that Overman, Owens, Tatum, and I bought for him, pinned on him, and paid him a salary for wearing . . . to keep things in hand . . . not crime, friend Ace, you know that, not crime . . . just the drunks swept up, and a check on impulsive gunplay—"

Poole sighed. "Now we have our hired marshal becoming a real lawman. Overman and Bat Owens did not object? . . . Thought so. . . . Declaring we need a regular sheriff, a court. And my good customers, the Texans, brought it on. Mr. Crane, they could have fought you and your damned railroad farm land, in other ways. But Denbo gets drunk. His crew gets out of hand." He thumped the account book. "I have the feeling this will be the last year I'll be in business. The Texans have forced law and order—oh, and preachers and reformers on Olanthe. Why, Overman may never take a drink at the Texas, after this year! I hear a distant, but growing, call to other fields."

Ace blurted out, "What kind of answer is that?"

"Mr. Crane can explain, since I think he now has an ace for his hole card. As for your question— to be specific, I have not seen Denbo or Malan today, and, as of this moment, I hope never to see them again."

"Why didn't you say so?"

Poole smiled. "I did."

Larry stood up. "Maybe we'd better get to the other places, Ace?"

The marshal rose, keeping his eye on the gambler. "If either of them shows up—"

"Now, don't ask me to help you, Ace. If you're

going to make that badge legal, do it on your own, and all by yourself. In fact, I might even warn them you're looking for them."

"That way means trouble for you, Poole."

"Not really, Ace. Now, how could you arrest me?" He waved toward the door. "Good evening, gentlemen."

Out on the street, Ace asked, "What was all that talk about?"

"It wasn't talk—it was prophecy."

"You make less sense than he did."

Their next target of inquiry was a dilapidated hotel, down the row. It turned out to be an odorous barn, with a cracked mirror in the lobby. The squint-eyed clerk hated the world and, especially, Ace. But grudgingly, he informed them that Pardee Malan might be in his room.

"Knock. If he don't answer, just push in. There ain't any locks."

They went upstairs, and found their way down a dark, narrow corridor to a door with the number painted sickly green. Ace repeated his knock, and then, hand at his holster, opened the door. The room was empty; a box of a place with an iron-frame bunk and a rag of a rug on the splintered floor. A saddle roll stood in one corner.

Ace pointed to it. "At least he's in town."

"But no sign of Denbo."

Ace spun on his heel, and led the way back

downstairs, to the squinting clerk. "Tell Malan I want to see him, pronto."

"Now I can't watch for every—"

"You'll watch for this one, friend. Else, tomorrow morning, you'll find yourself closed for the rest of the year. Savvy?"

The man nodded, growling in his throat. Ace slapped his hand on the counter to accent his threat. He nodded to Larry, and they left.

Two more gambling spots declared that they had seen neither of the two Flying W men. Coming out of the last place, Ace indicated the row of shacks beyond. "Leaves just the girls down here."

"Could be a waste of time. Anyhow, you'll see them all on your rounds, won't you?"

"Make a point of it," Ace said, relieved. "If I find either of those two, where will you be?"

"At the hotel. But I'll check with you down here, later tonight."

Larry walked back to the railroad station, where Ross was all excited questions about the fire. "Now, don't tell me you ain't got an idea who done it! I've heard how that Flying W segundo—and Denbo—kicked threats around last night. It was one of them."

Larry asked sharply, "Malan, too?"

"Well . . . Malan sent a telegram down to Texas half an hour ago. Can't say what it was, of course, but him and Denbo—nope, better shut my mouth."

Larry pressed, but Ross would not talk, despite Larry's coaxing that they both worked for the railroad company. "Now, Larry, you know I got principles, as well as rules. No difference what Malan said in a telegram than what Overman might order by wire. Both confidential—and I'll stick by that, even if they fire me for it."

Larry bowed to the inevitable. "Can you send a telegram to Marlowe, Chicago office, as I talk it?"

"I got a fast key."

Larry stepped into the office, and Ross sat before the key, signaled the Chicago office code, and looked up at Larry. "Start talking."

Ross kept the chattering code flowing over the wires, as Larry dictated his intentions to rebuild his office and conduct business from Blaine's hotel. Ross winced when Larry concluded that he, and such law as there was in Olanthe, were hot on the lookout for Denbo and Malan.

Ross dropped back in his chair, at the last click of the key. "About Malan—maybe you'd better not be too sure. I know I ain't, after hearing what you just sent. He's around town, Larry."

"Then tell me what he sent."

"Can't—just can't, Larry. Like I wouldn't tell him what you just sent."

Larry left the station, and walked toward the hotel. He stopped for a look at the cold ashes of what had been his office, then he moved quickly on. He stepped briskly up on the hotel porch, and started across it.

A figure materialized in the doorway, and Larry stopped short. Pardee Malan stood framed, his right hand hanging at his side, just below his Colt.

"I've been waiting for you, Crane."

# XV

Larry inched his hand up toward his own gun, but Malan warned, with the ghost of a smile, "No gunplay, Crane. I want to talk to you, not kill you."

Larry did not lower his hand an inch. "About raids? Burning? Murder?"

"That's why you're looking for me, ain't it? Word came to me. Yes, about that—and Brace Denbo." Malan gestured toward the end of the porch. "We can talk there."

Malan moved out of the doorway, and sauntered toward the far railing. Larry followed him. Malan reached the railing, and waited for Larry. "First, don't get the idea that I've changed my mind about you. But that can wait."

"You said this was about Brace."

"It is, but I don't want you reading my brand wrong. Brace has gone loco—plain out of his head. First, he had you figured, but you wouldn't listen to reason. Then there was that girl in the railroad car. He thought he had her figured, too."

"He should've known better, I could've told him."

Malan knifed a smile at Larry. "No man asks another if he's making a fool of himself, and that's what Brace did."

159

Larry asked impatiently, "Is this what you want to talk about?"

"No, but it explains me—to you. And maybe it tells you why I'm going to say what I've done, and plan to do. First, I tried to sober Brace up, and talk some sense in his head. I guess neither was right-possible. He couldn't forget the way that girl laughed in his face."

"She said she tried to be gentle, that she never led him on."

"She lied, on both counts—and you just have to look at her to know it. Anyhow, he figured to tally on her and you and the railroad, all at once. I figured I'd brought him around to some kind of straight thinking, but he broke away from me. First thing I know, he's ordered the crew to saddle up and—well, by now, you know the rest."

Larry studied Malan with a level eye. "You're saying you had nothing to do with the raids?"

"That's exactly what I'm saying. I took him to the camp, and he was acting and talking sane. At least, I figured he was mainly over his crazy fit. So I come back here."

Malan waved a finger toward the girl-shacks, and smiled knowingly. "I had someone waiting for me down there, no matter how late I got back. First time I knowed anything was wrong was when she woke me up, and told me your office had burned down. I figured it was an accident until I heard about the raids and the shooting. I

160

skedaddled to our camp. Brace was gone. Crane, Brace Denbo ordered that shooting. Some of the boys sort of faded out of the firelight, but the rest . . ."

Malan paused, and went on. "Well, like me, none of 'em lost any love for a sodbuster, and that Briggs tried to set a rifle toll on our cattle. The boss gave the orders, and I don't blame 'em for liking the idea."

"But you didn't?"

Malan growled at the naked sarcasm in Larry's voice. "No! I come back, and couldn't find Brace. I sent a telegram back home."

"I heard about that."

"Then you know what I said?" Malan narrowed his eyes while Larry shook his head. "I told the boss what had happened. I said Brace had gone crazy, and Flying W was in trouble unless someone took over. You can ask Ross."

Malan pulled a folded telegram from his shirt pocket. "Here's the answer. Just came."

He held it out, and Larry took and read it. "Brace fired. Send him home. Take charge of trail crew. Help authorities straighten up mess. If Brace arrested, arrange bail or lawyer. If not, send him home. Tied up if you have to. You are in charge. Keep me posted. Lew Richards."

Larry handed back the telegram. "All right, I accept that. Now what?"

Malan folded the telegram, and put it back

into his pocket. "I help how I can—you and Ace Clemson. Understand, you and me have a score to settle, but it can wait—even to next year, depending on how this works out."

"I understand, Malan. But I don't know what you intend to do about Brace—or the fire and the murder of Briggs."

"Nothing—except find Brace before he does more damage." Worriedly, Malan rubbed his hand along his jaw. "I can't depend on most of my crew, Crane. I'll be honest. They'd buck me—and mainly because of you and them farmers."

"Then—?"

"I got friends among every trail-crew in Olanthe, right now. If you and Ace agree, I'll round 'em up, and that'd be a posse of sorts. We can comb every damn hole in town. Find Brace. That's first. After that, I leave it to Ace."

Larry stabbed at the floor with his toe. "Why did you come to me?"

Malan sounded disgusted. "You're hard to persuade! Mule-headed, like I figured!"

"Leave me out. Answer the question."

"Why—because you're mule-headed? If I showed up with Ace first, you'd buck, and we'd waste time arguing. This way, you know. How about it? Not that I won't help Ace, whatever you say, but you got your chance to say it—first."

"We need all the help we can get. So—I accept, but I'll keep an eye on you."

"Let's see Ace, then. And keep watching me, all you damn please."

Warily, side by side, they crossed the street to the marshal's office. Malan told Ace his story, and produced the telegram. Ace read it, asked a few questions and, after a confirming nod from Larry, said, "When can you get your bunch together?"

"Give me five minutes to get more cartridges, and maybe a rifle. Fifteen minutes after that, I'll meet you in front of the Texas, with twenty or more men."

Ace nodded, looked at Larry. "How about you?"

"Give me five minutes, too. I'll be back here."

Out on the street, Malan continued at Larry's side toward the hotel. Larry stopped short. "I thought you stayed down—"

"I stay here—in Denbo's room. I'm trail boss now."

"Did Miss Kathy—?"

Malan grinned. "Oh, she was upset a little, but she'll get over it. Nothing else she can do, is there?"

Larry's temper rose suddenly. "Leave her alone."

"To leave you with open range? Crane, have you figured you might end up like Denbo did with that one in the railroad car?"

Larry bristled with outrage. "Don't be a damn fool!"

"Why, I ain't. But have you asked her?

Something to think about, friend. Brace didn't, and that was his mistake."

Together, the two mounted the hotel steps, and crossed the porch. In stiff silence, they went upstairs and Malan turned off to his room, without a word.

Larry stayed in his room just long enough to take a box of cartridges from a drawer, and empty them into his pocket. Out in the hallway, Malan was not in sight. Larry hurried to the rear stairway, which led down to the first floor, just off the kitchen. As he peered into the kitchen, Kathy glanced up from the table where she was scribbling a grocery list. The pencil dropped from her nervous hand.

"Have you heard from Brace?"

"No, but Malan has his room here. Why did you permit it?"

"What could I do! He said he was the new trail boss, and that Mr. Denbo was missing, and in trouble. He—well, he just moved in, and there was nothing I could do about it."

Larry sighed. "I suppose not, without having trouble. But, Kathy, watch him and be careful. Don't hesitate to call for me or Ace Clemson, if Malan gets out of line. Promise?"

"Of course! But—what about Mr. Denbo? Is he all right? I can't believe he's done all those dreadful things."

Larry was impressed by the real concern in her

whole bearing. He answered gently, "Talk is one thing, fact another. We're looking for Denbo, to get his side of the story."

"But you believe he did set the fire and all those things?"

"Let's say his going into hiding is highly suspicious."

Down the short hallway from the kitchen, Larry walked to the lobby. Kathy's worried face was fixed in his mind as he hurried on to the Texas Saloon.

Ace Clemson was waiting. Ace grunted acknowledgement of Larry's presence, and continued looking out the window for Pardee Malan. At the appointed time, an assortment of cowboys came striding from the saloons, with Malan at their head. "Will these do the job for you, Marshal?"

Ace nodded. "So long as they take orders from me."

"They will. Give 'em."

Ace divided the men into small groups, and gave each the task of combing a specific area, nor did Ace neglect the pens beyond the railroad station, nor any of the old camping grounds of the trail-herds. Before taking leave, each group looked to Malan for confirmation, which he gave with a nod. Finally, only Malan and two others were left.

"What about me, Marshal?"

"You three cover the shacks, one at a time. Crane and me will search the livery stable and the outbuildings, along Main Street. If you turn up anything, you'll find one or the other of us, up that way."

Malan raised his hand in a half-salute, then wheeled about and left, the two men following. Ace and Larry headed toward the main street. Around the corner, Larry remarked, "Notice how those cowboys looked to Malan for orders?"

"Sure. He's their kind. I don't entirely trust Malan, but I'll work with anyone who'll turn up Denbo, and end this business." Ace indicated the buildings behind the livery stable. "Work up that way, Crane, back of the stores. Denbo could be anywhere in that jumble of sheds."

They separated. Larry dove into the open stretch beside the stable.

He directed his attention to a small shed, just ahead. Larry loosened his Colt in its holster, and kept his hand close to it as he stole up toward the shed, his eyes sweeping every crack between the warped boards. He put his hand cautiously on the door knob, and threw open the door. The shed was empty, except for some burlap sacks on the dirt floor. He left the shed, and moved toward the larger buildings behind Overman's store.

Overman appeared at the rear door. "Crane, the place is locked tight. Ace told me about Denbo, but there's no chance he's in any of my buildings."

Larry glanced inside, past Overman. "Fine, Harry, but get the keys, and let me make sure. It'll make us all feel better, including you."

Overman grumbled, but went, and came back with a ring of keys. He started off left, toward the first of his three shanties, but Larry stopped him. "Harry, suppose Denbo is in there somewhere, with a gun in his hand? Maybe, I'd better do the looking."

Overman handed him the keys, and retreated to his doorway. He waited nervously till Larry emerged from the last of the three shanties, and brought back the keys. "All clear."

Larry left Overman, and went next door, to the coal shed behind the saddleshop. The coal shed produced nothing, and Larry worked his way northward. He was inside a tumble-down structure when he heard a step outside. He whirled, his Colt jumping into his hand.

In the doorway appeared one of Malan's cowboys. He stopped short on perceiving the leveled gun, then recovered with a grin. "Hate to run up against your gun, Crane, but Pardee thinks we've found Denbo, and sent me to find you."

"Where?"

The cowboy yanked his thumb in the direction of the huts beyond the honkytonks. "Mex-Indian gal over there has been hiding him. Pardee found out about it, down on the row."

Larry's eyes lit with excitement. "Get Ace."

"I done that, down at the livery corral. Ace told me where to find you, and said for you to hurry over."

Larry brushed past the puncher, and around the corner of the shanty. Dusk was casting long shadows over the grass that swished against his boots.

Eagerly, he scanned the silent fronts of a huddle of huts before him. On closer approach, the huts seemed to crouch down, like beasts lying in wait. Larry halted to reconnoiter. One hut was directly ahead, another off to his left, while a third hut stood further off at his right, close to the larger saloons. Larry looked back for the puncher, who was nowhere in sight. Larry turned again toward the huts, his fingers tightening over his gun. Ahead, the door opened slowly, and a man called, "Crane! Over here! We've been waiting for you."

It sounded like Malan. Larry went into a crouch, his eyes questioning the hut at his left, silent and brooding, where Denbo, no doubt, was lurking. Through the thickening twilight, Larry leapt toward the sanctuary ahead.

A tongue of orange-red flame lanced from the left hut, and the bullet zinged wickedly past his cheek. Gun in hand, he dropped to the ground, trying to get an aim on something, as a second gun spat from the left hut.

Larry yelled, "Malan! Ace! Cover me!"

# XVI

The two guns, together, sought out Larry as he lay in the tall grass. He fired two shots at the hut window. He heard the tinkle of broken glass and the muffled scream of a woman. He rolled sideways as slugs cut at him again, then he rose slowly, intending to dash for the half-open door ahead.

Then a gun blasted from the door, the slug tearing through Larry's sleeve. For a split second, he stood frozen in amazement, and then threw himself down and aside, as the third gun blasted again. He got a shot off at the spurt of flame in the doorway. A second later, a man pitched through the door, his knees crumpling, his revolver spilling from his fingers. Larry turned and fired twice toward the hut at his left, then raced forward in a crouch. He jumped over the body on the low porch, and plunged through the doorway.

The interior was dim. Dresses hung along a wall, and beneath them, on a cot, lay a figure. A door, in back, led to a room beyond. To his right, something moved, and he swung his gun around to fire.

A woman screamed. Larry jerked up the gun muzzle, and saw her crouching terrified under the window. Her eyes were wild, and her black hair streamed down over her shoulders. At Larry's approach, she shrank back.

"It's all right. I won't hurt you."

She screamed again, clawing at him with her fingers. He reached through her flying nails, and got in a good slap on her face. His slap took the hysteria out of her.

"I won't hurt you. Understand? Stay down. Where's Brace Denbo?"

She put out a trembling hand toward the figure on the cot. Larry went to the cot, and bent down to see who it was. He saw a face plastered with sweat, the jaw lolling, and the hair tousled. Denbo, all right—and then Larry's boot-toe spurned a bottle, that went rolling across the floor, with the growl of distant thunder. Denbo slept in a drunken stupor.

Quickly, Larry stepped to one side of the open door. He had a view of the darkening approach to the hut.

Larry ejected the empty shells from his Colt, and thumbed fresh rounds into the chamber. He clicked back the hammer, and lifted the muzzle, preparing to deal with a suspicious sound outside.

The woman whispered hoarsely across the room. "*Senor! Por Dios.* Let me go!"

"Stay down. You'll be killed."

"Ai-eee!" She made a choked cry, and muttered a prayer in rapid Spanish.

170

His eyes never budged from the open doorway as he strained to catch a repetition of the sound. Suddenly, Denbo stirred, and mumbled a curse. He gathered up his legs, pushing his boots onto the floor.

Just then, a figure flitted through the darkness beyond the door. Larry heard racing boots, and then a gun blasted, the bullet smashing into the far wall. Denbo's curse was drowned by the roar of Larry's gun.

One by one, his gun sought the men behind the gun-flashes out there in the ever-deepening darkness. A stream of bullets thudded into the door frame. A yell of agony outside answered Denbo's sudden cry of pain. Denbo slid off the cot, and struck the floor with a force that shook the flimsy walls. Denbo lay, breathing raggedly.

From the distance came shouts—help was coming. He listened hard, finger on the trigger. There was a scamper of boots off beyond the left hut, then all was still again.

Hoofbeats sounded up, then the thud of men jumping from their horses. Then a voice pierced the darkness. "This is the law! Show yourselves! Make a light! Or we'll be coming in, shooting!"

Larry stepped over the body in the doorway, and shouted, "Ace! This is Larry Crane. It's over. Come in. I'll find a light."

He turned to the sobbing woman beneath the

window. "Get up. It's over. Light the lamp. Hear me!"

Moving automatically to his command, she went into the further room. She exclaimed with fright as she stumbled, and then a match flared.

She returned with a lamp, its soft light filling the room. Boots hurried across the low porch, and Ace Clemson strode into the room. Other men, guns in hand, pressed in behind him.

Lamplight revealed the woman as fairly young, but her dark face was ravaged by hunger, dissipation, and fear. Ace Clemson knelt beside Larry, and turned Denbo over.

Blood was spreading from Denbo's left shoulder, down over his chest. Denbo's eyes were shut, and the booze-flush had drained from his face. Ace sprang to his feet.

"Rip up a sheet. We'll have to stop that bleeding, pronto."

Larry looked about, pulled the rumpled sheet from the cot, and tore it into strips. Men knelt beside the body in the doorway, and dragged it to one of the horses. Someone said, "There's a man dead, out here in the yard."

Larry helped Ace bind Denbo's wound. At last, Ace hunkered back on his heels, and swiped his shirt sleeve across his sweating face. "We've stopped the blood."

"Will he live?"

"It'll be nip-and-tuck, what with no doctor in

town. Maybe a nurse would help some, if we can find one. In any case, we better get him out of here."

He signaled two men, watching from the doorway. "Go to Overman's. Tell him we want something to make a stretcher, and get back here as soon as you can."

The two hurried out, and a man came in. He gestured toward the dark yard. "Marshal, two dead men laid out on the porch, and a woman next door, with a bullet gouge in her arm. This was one hell of a gun fight."

Ace nodded grimly. "Who are the men?"

"Texans. The one shot in here was from Flying W. Him and that Pardee Malan was always together at the Texas, or at Dick Poole's. The other'n is from another crew, but—"

"Friend of Malan's," Larry cut in.

The marshal turned sharply. "Where's the woman?"

Larry wheeled, and dove into the rear room just as the rear door opened, and the woman's dark figure flitted into the night. Larry and Ace ran after her.

Larry caught up with her. Screaming, she whirled and clawed at him. Her right fingers raked his face as he grabbed her about the waist, pinioning her arms. She kicked at his shins savagely until Ace came up and helped subdue her.

They pulled and pushed her back into the shack, and sat her on a chair. She rubbed her arms, and glared defiantly, first at Ace, and then at Larry. Ace pointed to Denbo's bandaged figure, on the floor.

"He set a gun-trap here, didn't he?"

"I know nothing—nothing at all."

"You'd better know something fast, Señorita, or you'll land in jail for a long, long time."

She glowered even more fiercely. Larry said, "Ace, you asked the wrong question."

"What do you mean?"

"I'm not sure but—" He turned to her, and asked quietly, "How long has he been here?"

Her dark eyes threw sparks, and she answered sullenly, "Two days, now."

"Night before last—when he came, was he sober?"

"No, but he had not—how you say?—passed out. He wanted to fight someone—maybe, two or three. One of them was a woman."

Larry shot a look at Ace, who listened, frowning. "He came alone?"

"No. There was another. But he left." She bobbed her head at Denbo scornfully. "I was to keep this one drunk, and not let him leave. It was not hard to do."

"The man who shot at me—and those in the next house—when did they come?"

"Late this afternoon."

Larry peered at Ace, and said quietly, "Now comes the key, Ace. Brace yourself." He turned to the girl. "The man who brought Denbo, and told you to keep Denbo drunk here, and the one who brought the gunmen later was the same?"

"*Si.*"

"Pardee Malan?"

"*Si!*"

"I'm damned!" Ace growled.

"No, Ace. But it was planned for Denbo and for me—and, maybe, a few others. Now, a question for you, Ace—did Malan send word to you that Denbo was here?"

"No. First I knew anything was going on was when I heard shots up this way. I didn't know Denbo was anywhere around."

"But Malan sent a man to tell me, Ace. I was suckered into a gun-trap."

The marshal pulled off his hat, and rubbed his hand distractedly through his hair. He looked down at Denbo and grunted, "So we hunted the wrong men—and the right man was with us the whole time, and making us believe his lies. But why?"

Larry sighed. "I have an idea, but there's no use guessing. We had guesses about Brace—and how wrong were they? If he was here all the time, he couldn't have killed Briggs, shot up both farms, and set fire to my office. The girl here is proof of that."

Just then, steps sounded on the porch, and three men came in, one of them carrying a stretcher made from a sawed-up pole, with canvas cut to fit. Carefully, Larry and Ace moved Denbo onto the stretcher. Ace ordered the men to carry Denbo to his room in the hotel, but Larry objected.

"Until we find Malan, Denbo won't be safe—or the girl here."

Ace grunted in comprehension. "Take 'em both to the jail."

With a cry, the woman sprang from the chair, and darted toward the door. Larry caught her arm, and spun her into the marshal's arms. She subsided again into sullen silence, and Ace led her out the door, after the men with the stretcher.

It was pitch-dark. Someone had brought a lantern, and it bobbed ahead of the stretcher-bearers as they trudged toward the main street and the jail. Now and then, one of the men would stumble and curse, and Ace's voice would rise sharply, cautioning against jarring Denbo.

From the main street appeared a flock of lanterns, as the roused citizens fell in line to volunteer their help. Nothing less than a festive procession finally turned into the main street, with every building lit up in celebration.

Fifty yards from the jail, a girl forced her way through the crowd to the stretcher. The bearers stopped. It was Kathy, the flooding light showing up the drawn lines on her face, and the pools of fear that were her eyes. She clapped a hand to her mouth to muffle a cry as she bent her gaze on Denbo's pale face.

She saw Larry, and reached toward him. "Is he—badly hurt?"

"Yes. We need a doctor but—"

"I'll nurse him. Take him to the hotel and—"

Ace intervened gently, explaining that Denbo would be safer in jail, though not mentioning Malan. Kathy's face twisted in anguish, but she acquiesced instantly. "Anywhere! Just so we get him well. Let me go home for the things we'll need. I'll be right back."

She broke a path back through the crowd while Larry followed the stretcher-bearers into the jail. From the front office, a door opened on a corridor leading to two opposite cells. Ace swung open the barred door of the cell at the right. The two bearers entered, and transferred their unconscious burden onto the bunk.

Ace unlocked the cell at the left, ejected a drunken puncher, and put the Mexican girl in there. For half a minute, she stood grasping the bars and spitting oaths in Spanish, but then she slumped onto the bunk, and watched the corridor with smoldering hatred and occasional muttered threats.

Kathy came hurrying down the corridor, carrying a basket of bandages and ointments. She brushed the men aside, pushed into the cell, and bent over Denbo. "I'll need clean, hot water to rinse the wound. Is the bullet—?"

"No need to worry—it went clean through," Ace answered quickly. "Out the side in the back."

She nodded crisply. "Now, gentlemen, if you'll clear out, and leave me room to work . . ."

Ace herded the onlookers down the corridor and out onto the street. He closed the door on them, and locked it, then turned with a sigh to Larry. "Now, what about Malan?"

"By now he'll know. He won't stay in Olanthe, and he'll leave as quickly as he can get—" Larry's hand shot to the door-key. "I'm going to the hotel. Malan stayed in Denbo's room."

"And you ain't going alone," Ace snapped.

They stepped outside, and brushed aside half a dozen questioners as they crossed the street. At the hotel, they stopped in the lobby, and listened. A deathly hush permeated the building. Larry led the way upstairs, and down the hall to Denbo's room. Outside the door, they drew their guns.

Ace flung his shoulder against the door, and lunged flat against the wall inside the dark room. Larry stood by the door, glancing up and down the hall. In a minute, Ace said, "Empty. Wait'll I light the lamp."

They bent their heads into every cranny. Signs showed that someone had hastily come and gone, for dresser drawers were pulled out, and Malan's saddle roll was gone. Larry holstered his gun.

"He's headed for the Flying W camp. But he won't be there long before he cuts south to Indian country. We might catch him at the camp."

"I'll get horses. We'll ride, pronto."

Larry agreed. "I have a rifle in my room. Meet you at the stable."

Ace hurried off while Larry closed Denbo's door, and walked to his own room. He opened the door, stepped inside, and moved toward the lamp on a table, across the room. Suddenly he sensed a presence in the darkness behind him. He started to turn.

The hard, round muzzle of a gun jabbed into his back.

# XVII

"I'm going to kill you, Mr. Crane."

The youthful voice broke from a cross between a baritone and a high tenor. The gun bored into Larry's back. Lamplight, streaming in from the corridor, cast two blending silhouettes on the window wall.

Larry stood still and interrogated the voice, which was certainly familiar. "Why kill me?"

"Because you're to blame, Mr. Crane. Dad would be alive now, if it hadn't been you got him out here. You didn't shoot him but—"

The gun muzzle dug deeper. Larry stood frozen. "Why am I to blame, Luke?"

The voice broke, sobbing softly. "Like I said, it was you and that damn railroad brought him out here. It was you made him drop this very rifle when he could've killed those cowboys. Then they killed him!"

"But I didn't, Luke." Ever so slowly, Larry rose on his toes. "In fact, I came in to get a rifle and the marshal to go after the man who did."

"Lot of good that'll do Dad! He's dead! Buried!"

The muzzle gouged, and Larry eased ever so gently away from it. "Luke, wouldn't you like to see the real killer get caught?"

"Sure! and I aim to—even if I have to do it myself. But, first—you."

"I tried to keep your father from buying that land he did, Luke. Surely, you know that?"

"You're trying to put the blame on Dad." The youthful voice broke in fury. "Don't try to clear yourself. Don't lie now! You're going to die in the next minute, Mr. Crane. That's a fact."

The gun muzzle slammed into the center of the small of Larry's back. Slowly, Larry raised his arms, crooking his elbows back. He heard the sob building in Luke's throat, that would tighten his finger on the trigger.

Larry came up on the balls of his feet, and he whipped about, his elbow knocking aside the gun muzzle. The rifle roared, and the dresser mirror went crashing.

Larry continued his swing to the right, all the way round. He saw Luke's round, pale eyes. Then his left fist, with all the power he had, cracked into the boy's jaw, and his right hand grabbed for the rifle barrel.

Larry snatched away the weapon as Luke went reeling back and down. He struck the edge of the bed, hung limply a moment, and then rolled out on the floor.

Larry gazed down at Luke, and suddenly everything drained out of him. He lowered his arms and, still holding the rifle, dropped on the bed. Beads of ice stood out on his forehead.

He sat up, and took several deep breaths, then pumped the rifle lever, emptying the chamber. The bright cartridges dropped in a heap on the dull green carpet. Larry studied the rifle in his hands, and then took it to the open window. He brought back his arm, and hurled the rifle far out. It struck the porch roof, and clanked to a stop against the eaves.

As Larry turned, Luke twitched, then moaned, and he opened his eyes blearily. He remained still, staring up at Larry with the eyes of a schoolboy in terror of the rod.

"On your feet, Luke. I'm not going to hit you. Sit over there."

Luke scrambled to his feet, and dropped into the chair. He sat, arms between his legs, watching Larry with a hangdog look. Larry strode slowly to the window and back, then sat on the corner of the bed.

"Luke, you're lucky. You nearly did something that would've haunted you the rest of your life. Murder, Luke, let that sink in . . . murder . . . in cold blood. How does it sound, said that way?"

Luke's eyes filled with tears, that went rolling down his cheeks.

Larry softened his voice. "I know how you must have felt about your father. It was a terrible thing, but it twisted up your thinking, Luke. Had you killed me, do you think the marshal would have done nothing? Where would you be now? You'd be skulking through the shadows, Luke, trying to get away. You couldn't have gone home—and what about your mother and sisters, then? You couldn't really go anywhere, Luke—anywhere safe for you. Had you thought of that?"

Larry stood up, and walked to the window again, looking out into the night. Across the way, at Tatum's, Ace Clemson appeared, carrying a rifle, in the rectangle of yellow light before the open door, and then disappeared into the stable. Larry sat down again on the bed, and Luke, swallowing, hard, asked, "What are you going to do with me, Mr. Crane?"

"Nothing, Luke. Memory of this will be your own punishment. But I tell you what *I'm* going to do."

The boy's mouth jerked open. "Luke, I came here to get my rifle to help the marshal find your father's killer. In a minute, you and me will walk out of here. You're going home, and you're going to stay there until someone comes to see you tomorrow. Understand?"

The boy nodded, making no sound. Larry pointed a long finger at him. "If you're not there, I'm changing my mind about you. This was attempted murder, and I'll tell the marshal, and ask that you be arrested."

Luke's face wried with dismay, but Larry swiftly continued. "But if you are there, no one but you and I will ever know about tonight. I have plans for you, Luke, that fit right in with what your Dad would have wanted. You'll stay on that farm. You'll work it. You'll support your mother and sisters. Someday, soon, this whole country will be farms, and I have plans for you even then."

Larry stood up. "You'll have proved yourself by then, I hope. So I'm planning on you to become a leading citizen. You'll help build this country into one of the richest farm areas in the whole United States—you and Jory Whelan and his dad. That's what I plan for you."

Luke blinked, and then his face cleared very slowly, and came alight with a glow from deep inside. "You really mean it, Mr. Crane?"

"Every word. Now on your feet, and out of here. I have things to do. I'll see you in the morning."

Larry turned his back on Luke, and went to the closet, opened it, and took out a hunting rifle. He jacked a shell into the chamber and then, glancing round, saw Luke Briggs, still in the chair.

"Luke, I said to go."

The boy rose awkwardly to his feet, shifted his weight, and said, "I near did a crazy thing, Mr. Crane. I want to thank you for stopping me."

Larry smiled wanly. "Amen to that!"

He pushed the boy ahead, into the corridor, and went down to the lobby. Across the street, Ace was waiting with saddled horses. Larry turned to Luke.

"I'll trust you to go home—straight home. I'll bring your rifle tomorrow."

Then Larry hurried across the street. Ace grunted with relief as Larry came striding into the circle of lamplight. "Begin to figure Malan had trapped you."

"Not him. We'll be lucky to catch him."

Larry walked to the bay, shoved his rifle into a saddle scabbard, and lifted his foot to the stirrup. Ace watched, a half-formed question on his lips, then shrugged, and swung into the saddle. He neck-reined about to face Larry. "We'd be smart to have a posse with us."

"Deputize me, and that's enough. It'd take too long, and a bunch of riders will slow us up. Malan may be counting on that delay."

"Then—let's go find him."

They circled the railroad station and the pens, and headed out along the beaten, old cattle trail. Larry watched ahead for the red dot that would mark the Flying W campfire. Ace called, above the whistling wind, "We could be riding wild, Crane. Malan might hole up in town."

"Where? He'd be seen, and you'd get the word."

"He's got friends."

"Not everyone. Even he told me some of the crew were against raiding. He put Denbo in his place when he told it, though."

Larry pointed to a wink of light. "Up ahead.

We'd better drift in. Malan could have a trap set."

Ace answered sourly, "I wondered when you'd think of that. Maybe circle, and come in slow and easy from another direction?"

"With you teaching me, Ace, I'll learn."

"If you live long enough—or me, for that matter."

They held their horses to a slower pace as they swung off the trail, making a wide circle. At last, the wink of the fire stood between them and Olanthe, and they turned their horses directly toward it.

Ace reined up, after a few yards. "Crane, we'd be fools to go in together. Move off, and then drift in. I'll show up first."

"Damned if you do!"

"Damned if I don't! Who wears the badge in this partnership?"

He rode off before Larry could answer, and the night swallowed him. Larry moved a hundred yards to the right, and then in toward the fire. The wink grew larger, and he saw men moving about it. He drew rein, and studied the still-distant figures.

They were standing in a group, facing a man whose back was to Larry. Now and then, he caught a word, then the voice was snatched by the prairie breeze.

Larry drew his Colt, spurred lightly, and the bay moved in. Now, he saw the fire-lit faces.

The man, who had his back to Larry, half-turned.

Pardee Malan—and in that second, his voice came clear. "You fools! I showed you Richards' telegram. I'm the boss. If you side with Denbo, you'll be fired as soon as the Boss hears about it."

Now, Larry perceived that the group beyond the fire was divided into two parts. A man spoke up, in the larger group, at right. "Pard, we don't believe that Denbo or Lew Richards wanted us to raid them farmers—and sure as hell, he don't want us to kill no marshal and land agent!"

"You heard Denbo—right here."

"He was drunk. Then you took him back to town—you and those special friends of your'n." The man swung his arm toward the smaller group, at left. "We had no part of it. Figure we lied for you when that land agent came asking questions, but that's as far as we go. Maybe you're the new trail boss, but this is one set of orders we ain't following. We're punchers, not gunslingers."

Larry discerned a shadow moving, ahead at left. Ace Clemson materialized, horse and man gigantic in the firelight. Larry touched a spur to his horse.

The marshal's voice rang like a bell. "Malan, I'm arresting you for half the crimes in the book."

# XVIII

No man moved. Malan's hand rose, and fell feebly as he swiveled his head, and stared. Larry worked his horse forward, till he was just outside the ring of light.

Ace held his gun on Malan, and spoke quietly. "Turn around, and back up to me, Malan. Keep your hands high, and in sight."

For a long moment, Malan stared at Ace, then slowly turned his back, lifting his hands shoulder-high. For a second, Larry could not see Malan's face as he turned his head toward his small group of supporters. Slowly, Malan took a step back, then a second.

Unseen behind the larger group, a puncher snatched his Colt from its holster, and it spat a flame at Ace. The bullet missed by a hair, and Ace swung his gun, and fired in the direction of the shot. The other punchers snapped out of their frozen stance as Malan spun about, dropping into a crouch, his gun magically in his hand. He snapped a shot at Ace, and the marshal's right arm dropped, his weapon flying from his fingers.

The Flying W's two factions turned on each other, and fought it out. Larry watched, trying to get his bearings.

The sight of Malan's gun, raised for a second

shot at the helpless marshal, snapped Larry out of his confusion, and he brought his gun down into aim. Then Malan flinched from a wild shot. Two of his pals were down, and the others whirled and fled, with Denbo's supporters in hot pursuit.

Malan panicked, and raced out of the light. Then he saw Larry directly in his path. Malan halted, and swung up his Colt. Larry's gun followed Malan in his flight, and steadied on his halting figure.

Both guns roared as one. A bullet sang past Larry's ear, and off into the night. Malan's chin jerked downward, and he spun halfway round, then tried to turn and lift his gun for a second shot. Larry took deliberate aim, and fired again. Malan fell backward, his arms flailing, and his gun making a fiery finger that traced an arc aloft, and disappeared into the grass.

A flurry of gunshots, then distant shouts, and then hoofbeats fading away, signaled the end of the fight. Larry sprang from his horse, looked down at Malan, and ran over to Ace, who was reeling in the saddle, his hand clutching his right shoulder, blood streaking along his fingers. He glared down at Larry. "Malan got away. Get him."

"He's back there. I got him."

Ace blinked, then leaned toward Larry, and toppled sideways. Larry caught Ace, and eased him to the ground. Then jumping shadows blocked the light from the fire, and men were standing in a half-circle around him and Ace. He started to raise his gun, but a man called out, "Hold it! We're on your side!"

The man who had defied Malan stepped up, and bent over Ace, asking, "Is he bad-hurt?"

"Shoulder. Bleeding." Larry waved an arm. "Malan's down out there. Bring him in."

Larry ripped the shirt from the marshal's wound, and put up the heel of his palm to restrain the show of willing hands. He tore a piece from his own shirt-front, and bandaged Ace's wound with it.

Then Ace opened his eyes, and pulled himself to a sitting position. He winced with pain, touched his shoulder, and looked surprised at the rude bandage.

Someone called, "Hey! Pardee took a bad one!"

Men brought Malan in, and placed him on blankets near the fire. Larry rose and saw three defeated men, standing under the guns of half a dozen victors. He hurried to Malan's side, and bent down. Someone had ripped Malan's shirt and underwear from his wound, and Larry clacked his teeth in dismay at the sight of it.

Just then, Malan opened his eyes and looked directly at Larry. With a quirk of his lips, he said, "So we had our showdown—you and me. Feels like your slugs left nothing below my chin."

"It's bad," Larry confided. "We'll try to get you to town and—"

"Won't make it—and what if I did?" Malan closed his eyes for a second, and Larry noted his glistening-white pallor, accented by the firelight. "You lose a game, you leave the table. Right?"

"What game were you playing—and why?" Larry asked.

Malan's eyes popped wide open with annoyance. "Don't you know, by now! I had a score to even—with you. There was Brace, too, but it wasn't the main thing with him. His job—trail boss . . ." His voice faded, then came back. "The way things went, they played just right. Your damn farmers . . . that woman who played Brace for a fool . . . you refusing to sell land. Then Brace got drunk, after the woman told him what a fool he was. He's trail boss . . . he has to keep everything in line. If he don't . . ."

Malan's voice faded to a whisper, and Larry bent to catch it. "That was a smart one, wasn't it? Boss a thousand miles away, and everything going to hell here. Pardee Malan the only one who . . . ah, but it didn't work."

One of the Flying W men broke in. "But most of those jiggers you gathered weren't Flying W—not us. Not unless Brace himself—"

"Shut up!" Malan gasped. "My friends hate sodbusters. So they helped me, and chased off the plowmen."

Larry shook his head. "You're a fool, Malan.

How about the marshal—and me? We'd have known."

"Dead? That was what I come out here for, tonight. Two bullets, that's all—and wrapped up. Overman, Owens, and their kind? Hell! they go along where they smell money coming, and—"

He groaned, and caught his breath. "You gone, Texas men riding high, they'd have said nothing. Backed me. It figured, and—who knows? That girl at the hotel—she might have come around to looking my—"

His lids weighed down, and his eyes shut. He breathed quietly for a moment, and then his throat filled with blood. He sat up choking, spat, struggled to catch his breath, and collapsed. A puncher said, "Looks like he's dead. I don't know whether to be sorry or not."

Larry bent over Malan, and moved his hand before Malan's eyes to test his sight. Then he stood up, looked down at Malan for a moment, and turned away. Ace Clemson sat by the fire, his bandaged arm now in a crude sling. Malan's three supporters still stood under guns, and Ace pointed them out as Larry came up.

"What about them? They helped raid and burn. We can jail 'em at Olanthe, and then, when I can ride, I'll take them east, to the nearest court. What do you say? You're one of the injured parties."

Larry walked toward the men, stopped a few paces away. They eyed him beatenly. Larry looked back at Ace, and then faced the men again. "You're all from Texas spreads?"

They nodded. "Horses here?" Again the nods, and one pointed into the darkness just beyond the firelight. "All right, head south—back to Texas. And don't show your faces in Olanthe ever again."

One answered surlily, "My saddle roll's back at the hotel."

"Well, you got a choice. Leave it and ride free. Go back for it, and land in jail—for the rest of your life. Or hang, for your part in a murder."

The man shifted uneasily. "I'll ride."

Larry signaled to the man who had spoken up for the Flying W. "See they ride south. Maybe, some of your boys could ride with 'em until daylight, and make sure they're still headed south?"

"Sure. But that one—" the man pointed—"he's one of our crew."

"Will he be, when Richards gets the true story?"

"Reckon not. All right, you tinhorn badmen. Hit the saddle!"

In a few moments, the sound of fading hoofbeats marked the cavalcade's departure southward. The remaining crewmen buried Pardee Malan. Ace insisted on riding, if someone would help him into the saddle. One of the punchers asked to ride back with them.

It was very late when the three saw the lights

of Olanthe. They rode directly to the jail, and the new puncher helped Ace dismount. Kathy Blaine was keeping vigil over Brace Denbo, but she came hurrying down the corridor when she heard them dismount. She looked at Ace's wound, put a fresh bandage on it, and sent him home, promising she'd look in on him in the morning.

Denbo still lay in a coma, but Kathy was sure his condition was improving. "He'll come around—soon, I hope."

"What about you? You can't stay here. I'll spell you."

"No, Mr. Crane. You're worn out. I can tell. Besides, I want to be right here when Brace—Mr. Denbo wakes up."

Larry studied her a second, and then shrugged. "See you in the morning then."

He slept late, and awakened in blazing sunlight. He dressed, and hastened to the jail, where he was amazed to find Ace in his office—sling and all.

Ace saw his concern. "Everything's fine now, Larry. Denbo came around, just before dawn. Might take a time for full recovery, but he's got a good nurse."

"Where is she?"

"I sent her home, and she was too dead on her feet to argue. You know, she's in love with that jasper. It shows like a new brand."

"With him!"

"Sure. Just watch her, next time you see them

together. And Denbo likes the idea, too. Want to see him?"

"I guess so."

"I been talking to him. He didn't know what Malan was doing. Whirling-drunk, when he wasn't passed out. Admitted that fine lady in the railroad car—well, he'll tell you. Anyhow, Malan told the truth."

Larry went with Ace to the cell. He found Denbo awake, more than willing to talk about Malan. "I knew he was a mean one, down underneath, when he was prodded. But to do this! I can't figure it. Are you sure he planned—?"

"Sure," Larry answered, and repeated the story, as Denbo listened with an amazement that would prove lifelong.

But during his recuperation—a few days in jail and then a few weeks in the hotel—he did come to believe. During that time, the last of the cattle-herds were driven up from the south, loaded into the cars, and hauled east. The crews had their wild time, and then departed, and Olanthe faced another year of emptiness.

But soon after, the westbound trains began to stop, and strangers descended, men with the mark of the farm and the plow on them. They asked their way to the rebuilt land office, and talked for hours with Larry Crane. Or he took them on long rides beyond the pens, southward over the railroad lands. More red rectangles appeared on the new map sent by the Chicago office.

Larry wrote Marlowe a long report. Marlowe's wires in reply became calmer, as Larry began to report the land sales.

Larry watched Kathy Blaine's growing devotion to Denbo. His own reaction surprised him. After his first twinges of jealousy, he was not heartbroken.

News came that a new western railroad was already in building. One night, at the Texas Saloon, Dick Poole looked around at the big, empty room and the few townsmen who gathered with him at the bar, Larry among them.

The gambler ordered Bat to serve drinks all around. "On me, gents, and for the rest of the evening. It's sort of thanks, and goodbye—thanks to Olanthe as it was, and goodbye to you gents who'll profit from what it will be. Me, I won't."

They stared, but Dick's skeletal features remained impassive until each man had his drink. Then came the chorus of questions.

Dick Poole looked at Larry with no animosity. "Why, it's that new railroad, down there. No trail drives here anymore, my friends. No wild punchers, drinking, gambling, and whooping it up. Larry here was right, but none of us believed him. Like you look at four cards of a spade straight, and you know the hole card don't fill it. But it did. You're smarter than us, Larry. Your health, if Bat will fill 'em up again."

They drank Larry's health, and Poole said, "Larry, reckon you could sell my building and the stuff in it? Appreciate it, if you would. If you can't, burn it. I've made a thousand times what the stuff cost me. Drunken punchers are lousy card players. Anyhow, I'm heading west—away from farmers. Not for me. I'll find some more punchers, or miners, or something."

"But—just like this, Dick?" Oberman demanded.

"Just like this, Harry. All the girls are gone, and they won't be back. The hotel down here will rot. You'll have a nice, clean town—with a courthouse, a church, a lodge, streets, and stores. There'll be church-socials and revivals. Now where in hell can you fit me into that! Your health, gents, and wish me mine—wherever I go."

Two weeks later, at the railroad station, Ross handed Larry a flimsy. "Glad for you, Larry, but damn sorry for me and the rest of us."

Larry stared, then read the flimsy—from Jepson Reeves. "Marlowe sending man to replace you. Meet me Denver soon as possible. Have arrangement concerning railroad land from Kansas to Coast that might interest you. See you Brown Hotel in few days. Harriet sends her regards. Jepson Reeves."

Larry's lips formed a soundless whistle as he slowly folded the telegram.

That evening, sitting with Kathy and Denbo on

the hotel porch, he showed the wire to Kathy. She read it, and her face lighted. She flung the wire into Denbo's lap, and turned, throwing her arms around Larry, and kissing him. "I'm so glad! It's a setup."

"Reeves doesn't say so."

"Larry Crane! What does 'Kansas to the coast' mean!"

"A lot of range to cover," Denbo said, and extended his hand. "And you sure got my best on that long trail."

Larry folded the wire, and put it in his pocket. "What about you two?"

Kathy blushed, and Denbo moved uncomfortably in his chair. "Well, we been talking, Larry, me and her and her mother. They figure they're tired of running a hotel, and I've told 'em about Texas—and Flying W—and my job down there. So, Kathy and me—we'll get married, and go back home."

Larry tested his reaction, for a split second. There was none. He extended his hand, as his other arm wrapped about Kathy, and he kissed the bride-to-be.

Two weeks later, after installing his replacement in the office, Larry threw his bags into the caboose of a westbound train. He shook hands with Ross, and stood on the rear platform as the conductor signaled the locomotive up ahead. The locomotive whistled. Harriet's face came clear in his mind's eye. Lovely woman—born flirt! Like the belles back in a vanished Virginia. She remembered him, sent her regards!

The train jerked, and the conductor swung aboard. He stood beside Larry as the train gained speed, and the station receded, Ross waving his farewell.

Larry had one last look at the town. The silent, doomed honkytonks, the shacks, the single street of small stores, Kathy's hotel dominating all the other buildings. Patternless, the whole.

"Olanthe ain't much," the conductor said, "but it's the last town between here and Denver."

"No, it ain't much," Larry agreed, adding softly, "but it will be."

"How do you know?"

"Know? I made sure of it!"

He turned, and entered the caboose, the puzzled conductor directly behind him.

Books are
produced in the
United States
using U.S.-based
materials

Books are printed
using a revolutionary
new process called
THINKtech™ that
lowers energy usage
by 70% and increases
overall quality

Books are
durable and
flexible
because of
smythe-sewing

Paper is
sourced using
environmentally
responsible
foresting methods
and the
paper is acid-free

**Center Point Large Print**
600 Brooks Road / PO Box 1
Thorndike, ME 04986-0001 USA

**(207) 568-3717**

**US & Canada:**
**1 800 929-9108**
**www.centerpointlargeprint.com**